I0835092

ISBN: 978-1-971734-08-8

This book is dedicated to those who have sent out a text or email in haste and paid the consequences for it. We all make mistakes!

Table of Contents

Sending It

Mia:

Ava had been part of my life for so long that sometimes I forgot I was allowed to be annoyed by her.

We lived three houses apart, which meant our moms knew each other, our dads did that awkward driveway wave thing, and for years it was assumed that if one of us got invited somewhere, the other probably was too. When we were younger, that had made us friends by default. Now it mostly made everything more complicated.

Ava had her group. I had mine.

The groups overlapped enough that we all ended up at the same birthday parties, sat near each other at lunch, and got stuffed into the same pictures at school events, but not enough that I told her everything or she told me everything. We were connected in that weird middle-school way where people could call you friends and still leave you out of half their lives.

Because she had always been there, Ava knew exactly how to get under my skin without even trying.

By the time I got home that afternoon, I was already in a bad mood.

I came through the front door with my backpack still hanging off one shoulder and one shoe half untied, then dropped everything by the stairs without bothering to put it away. My mom was in the kitchen unloading grocery bags and talking to me before I had even fully stepped inside.

"Mia, can you put the frozen stuff in the freezer?"

"In a second," I responded.

It came out in a tone I hadn't intended. I wanted to say, "I can't think about freezer waffles right now because the entire eighth grade has lost it."

My phone buzzed in my hand.

Buzzed again.

Then again.

My gaze dropped.

Becca: ***did you hear***

A second later:

no like what ACTUALLY happened

The screen glowed back at me.

All day, the rumor had been mutating like something alive.

At lunch, I heard Ava was crying in the girls' bathroom.

By sixth period, I heard Jayden had made her cry.

Ten minutes before the final bell, someone claimed Jayden had actually been defending her.

Somebody else said Ava and Jayden had been texting for weeks.

And now, according to three separate people and one very dramatic voice note from Becca, there had been some kind of scene after school involving Ava, Jayden, and enough weird energy to launch a thousand terrible group chat theories.

My mom shut the freezer door with her hip. "Mia?"

"Yeah, I heard you."

"Then please come and do as I ask."

I shoved two boxes of popsicles into the freezer without taking my eyes off my phone.

The thing about rumors at school was that they never arrived as one full story. They came in scraps. Fragments. Faces turning in the hallway. Half-heard whispers in line. Somebody swearing they knew for sure, which always meant they absolutely did not.

But no matter what version I got, Ava was in the middle of it.

That was Ava.

She had a way of ending up at the center of things. Not because she was loud. She was not one of those girls who shouted across the cafeteria or fake-laughed so everybody would notice her. It was more like drama gravitated toward her.

And now Jayden was involved too.

Which made everything that much worse.

Jayden was the kind of boy everyone liked, even when they tried not to. He was funny without being exhausting, cute without acting like he knew it, and the sort of person who could make a teacher laugh and get away with it. He was good at soccer, decent at school, and nice to everybody without seeming fake. Girls liked him. Boys liked him. Teachers liked him. Even my dad liked him and honestly, why not.

My phone buzzed again.

Becca: ***mia seriously call me***

Then: ***sophie said ava was literally crying***

I rolled my eyes so hard it hurt.

"How was school?" my mom asked.

"Fine," I said too quickly.

She gave me a look over a bag of grapes. "Yeah."

I ignored her and headed upstairs to my room, shutting the door with my foot.

The second I was alone, the pressure in my chest got worse.

That was the dumb thing. I knew I was too worked up. I knew it in the same way you know you should not keep poking a sore tooth with your tongue, except you do it anyway because your own self-destruction has somehow become interesting to you.

I sat on the edge of my bed, phone in both hands.

Another message from Becca appeared.

if ava is making this a whole thing again i swear

That did it.

Something hot and sharp rushed through me.

Not just because of Ava. Not just because of the rumor.

Mostly because it had been a long day and I was tired.

Tired of hearing her name every time anything happened.

Tired of everybody acting like she was always caught in the middle instead of maybe sometimes causing the middle.

Tired of how every story curved in her direction. And yes, if I was being honest, tired of seeing Jayden's name next to hers.

I was not in love with Jayden.

I barely even talked to him without other people around.

But he was the kind of boy you noticed. The kind of person everybody noticed. And if some weird story was suddenly wrapping itself around him and Ava, then the entire school had decided to care.

Including me.

Especially me, judging by the way my heart was beating.

I opened Becca's chat and started typing.

Fast.

Lightning fast.

The words came out hotter than I meant them to, but once they started, I did not slow down.

k im sry but ava is seriously exhausting

every week its some new drama but somehow everyones supposed to feel bad for her

and now jaydens involved too and honestly im not even surprised

if they want attention that bad then just say that

I read it once.

Not to edit it.

Just to admire how accurate it felt.

I hit send.

For one perfect little second, I felt better.

Lighter.

Like I had just gotten something off my chest.

Becca would text back something supportive, maybe add one more detail, maybe say exactly, and I would stop feeling like my ribs were wrapped too tight around my lungs.

The message appeared on my screen.

And my stomach dropped down to my toes.

It was not under Becca's name.

It was under our school's group chat — PANTHER PRIDE 8TH GRADE COMMUNITY.

I stopped breathing.

I mean I literally stopped.

My thumb jerked against the screen hard enough to almost drop my phone. My eyes locked on the top of the chat, willing the words to change, willing reality to develop an emergency reverse button just for me.

It did not.

No rescue. No reverse button.

The giant school group thread everyone hated until they needed it.

The one teachers used for reminders about assemblies and field trips and spirit week and missing lunch boxes and volleyball sign-ups and student council announcements. The one all of eighth grade was in. The one faculty checked. The one nobody was supposed to use for anything remotely interesting, which meant everybody checked it the second something remotely interesting happened.

And now, at the very bottom, glowing on my screen like a curse, was my message.

With Ava's name.

Along with Jayden's name.

With my own name stamped right above it for the entire grade to see.

"No," I gasped.

Panic hit me so hard I felt dizzy.

"No. No, no, no!"

I jabbed at the screen, opening the message fully like that would help. My hands were shaking so badly I hit the wrong thing twice. The chat loaded, and there it was again, even bigger now that I was inside it.

My message.

For all to see.

My face went hot all at once.

Maybe nobody had seen it yet.

Maybe I had time.

Maybe—

A new message popped up.

Ryder: wait WHAT

My entire body locked.

Another.

Sophie: mia omg

Another.

Derek: yoooo

I made a weird choking sound and scrambled off the bed so fast I nearly stepped on my backpack. I stood there in the middle of my room with my phone held inches from my face like maybe panic worked better at close range.

Delete.

I just needed to delete it.

I pressed on the message.

Nothing useful.

I pressed again.

Still nothing helpful enough.

Why were there seventeen different ways to react to a message and zero magical options for erasing this from existence and also wiping everyone's memory?

Another message appeared.

Ms. Ortega: Please keep this chat school appropriate.

That was the moment my soul tried to leave my body.

It wasn't other students.

It wasn't Ryder acting like he had just been personally gifted entertainment.

It wasn't even Sophie, who could probably smell drama from two zip codes away.

It was Ms. Ortega.

My English teacher.

My actual teacher had read it.

Which meant other teachers had probably read it too.

Which meant adults knew.

Which meant this was no longer embarrassing in a normal way. This was now embarrassing in a possibly-get-called-to-the-office way.

My phone buzzed so hard in my hand I almost threw it.

Becca calling

I hit decline instantly. I was in no mood to talk.

Then:

Becca: WHY WOULD YOU POST THAT ON THERE

As if I needed her help understanding the problem.

Another text from her.

Becca: MIA

Another.

Becca: CALL ME RIGHT NOW

My door cracked open.

"Mia?" my mom said. "Why are you stomping around like that?"

"What? Me?"

"Are you crying?"

"No!"

"Then why do you sound like that?"

Because my life is over, I thought.

Instead, I said, "Sorry I'll stop." Just to get her to leave me alone.

Which was such an obvious lie even I wanted to argue with myself.

My phone buzzed again.

This time I looked before I could stop myself.

The worst thing I had ever seen in my life.

Ava is typing…

I sat back down on the bed so hard the mattress springs squealed.

She stopped typing.

Started again.

Stopped.

Started.

Each set of bouncing dots felt like being slowly lowered into acid.

I could not decide what was worse: her answering in the chat where everyone could see, or sending me something private that would somehow be even angrier.

The dots vanished.

Nothing came through.

I felt worse.

Much worse.

Now I knew she had seen it.

And I knew she had started to type a reply and she had then decided not to.

My phone buzzed again.

A direct message this time.

From Jayden.

His name sat there, unopened.

My heart pounded so hard it blurred the edges of my vision.

Jayden had messaged me.

Jayden had read the message.

He had read it. Obviously.

The entire eighth grade had probably read it by now. Ninth and even seventh graders were probably reading it. Random parents were maybe reading it through older siblings who had taken screenshots. The message was probably already leaving school property.

I opened the thread anyway.

It was only four words.

what is this about

No emoji. No joke. No "lol." No softness at all.

I wanted the group to split open and take me.

Another message appeared in the community chat.

Assistant Principal Harlow: Mia, please report to the front office tomorrow morning before first period.

I shut my eyes.

Because why not, at this point? Why not make it official. This was no longer fixable. Not tonight.

Not fixable with a delete button, or a quick apology, or by throwing my phone out the window and pretending I lived in the eighteen hundreds.

Downstairs, my mom called, "Dinner in ten!"

I didn't answer.

I just sat there with my phone in my hand, my face burning, my stomach turning over itself, and the terrible understanding settling in piece by piece.

I had meant to send one angry message to one friend.

Instead, I had handed it to the entire eighth grade.

And tomorrow, I was going to have to walk into school knowing everybody had read exactly what I thought of Ava.

Or worse.

What they believed I thought of her.

The truth was, even now, with my pulse pounding and my teacher in the chat and the assistant principal involved and Jayden's message still open on my screen, one thought kept pressing through all the others:

What if the rumor was not even true?

That was when I finally felt sick.

Like really sick.

Not just embarrassed.

Not just panicked.

Just plain sick.

If I had just blown up my life over something half the school had made up between lunch and last bell, then this was not just a mistake.

It was my mistake.

And it was already way too late to take back.

Stress

Mia Continued:

It was a rough night. I barely slept. Every time I started to drift off, I saw it again.

My message, sitting there in the community chat like it had every right to exist.

Around midnight I checked to see if maybe I had dreamed the whole thing, which was both dumb and a little desperate. I had not dreamed it. It was still there, higher up now, buried under a pile of reactions, teacher reminders, and a Student Council message about spring fundraiser forms that felt almost offensive in its normalness.

Nobody had said anything official after Assistant Principal Harlow's message.

Not sure if that was good or bad.

By morning my stomach felt hollow and heavy at once, my emotions so raw that one wrong word might make me sob.

"Mia," my mom called from downstairs, "you're going to miss the bus."

I can't be seen like this. No way.

"I don't feel good!" I yelled back.

I needed a day to myself, but I knew my mom would never let me stay home unless I was visibly sick.

"You've missed too much school already. If you say you're sick I'll make you a doctor appointment!"

"Fine!" I called, mustering all the strength I had to crawl out of bed.

In the bathroom I brushed my teeth and made the mistake of looking up. I looked like somebody who had been caught shoplifting on the news. My hair was doing weird things. My eyes were puffy. My face looked guilty before I had even left the house.

At breakfast, my mom pushed a bowl of cereal toward me. "Everything okay?"

"Fine."

"You don't seem fine."

"It was a long night. I didn't sleep well."

She studied me over her coffee mug. "Did something happen at school yesterday?"

For one terrifying second, I thought maybe she had somehow seen the chat. Then I remembered she was not in it. Unless somebody's parent had screenshotted it and sent it around, which felt possible enough to make my pulse jump.

"No," I said, too fast again.

My mom raised one eyebrow. I hated how good moms were at hearing the lie even when they couldn't yet prove it.

"Well," she said, "if there's something going on you can talk to me."

I grabbed my backpack. "I'm late."

"Mia."

But I was already halfway to the door.

Outside, the air had that gray, cold morning feeling where everything looked flatter than usual. Our street was quiet except for the rumble of a garbage truck over by the corner.

And there was Ava, three houses away, standing at the end of her driveway.

Perfect.

For a moment I forgot everything. Even how to move.

She was with two girls from her inner group, Tessa and Lila, all three in hoodies and sneakers, backpacks hanging off one shoulder the exact same way. Tessa said something, and Lila laughed, but Ava wasn't laughing. She was looking at her phone.

She looked up.

Right at me.

My face went hot.

There are some moments where you can feel the exact second everything between two people changes shape.

That was one of them.

Ava didn't wave or smile.

I didn't either.

Tessa leaned closer and said something too quiet to hear. Lila glanced at me, then away, then back, the way people do when they're trying not to stare and failing.

I almost turned around and went back inside.

Instead, I walked.

Not toward them. Just down the sidewalk, trying to act like my life wasn't actively collapsing.

The closer I got, the quieter they became.

Ava's expression was not what I expected.

Not furious.

Just blank.

Which made her harder to read. It also helped me keep my own face in check.

"Mia," she said as I came level with them.

Her voice wasn't loud. It didn't need to be.

I stopped.

My heartbeat was probably loud enough to count as weather.

"Hey," I said, and immediately hated myself for choosing a word so normal.

Nobody said anything.

Tessa looked at Lila. "We'll meet you guys at school."

They left without another word.

Which I appreciated, except I also hated being left alone with Ava. Forced to face what I'd done.

She held her phone down at her side. "So."

That one word held more judgment than an entire paragraph.

My throat tightened. "Yeah."

"Were you going to talk to me," she asked, "or were you waiting for the office to do it first?"

That hit harder than I was ready for.

"Ava, I was in a mood and typed it out and sent it without thinking. I didn't mean what I said."

She stared at me.

She didn't believe me. The worst part was, I wasn't sure I believed me either.

"Ava—"

"I don't even care that you said it to Becca," she said, cutting me off. "I mean, I care, obviously. But whatever. People say things. I get that."

I blinked once.

That was not the direction I thought this would go.

She continued, her voice steady and clipped. "What I care about is that you said it like you know anything."

"I didn't mean—"

"You said I'm exhausting."

I winced.

"You said I drag people into things."

"Ava. I was frustrated. I'd been having a bad day."

"Yeah, I noticed."

A car rolled past and turned at the stop sign. Behind me, somebody's front door slammed. The neighborhood was waking up around us like this was an ordinary school morning, which felt rude.

Ava crossed her arms. "You could've just asked me."

About ten different answers rushed into my head, and none of them sounded good.

Instead, I said, "I know."

"That's it?"

"What do you want me to say?"

The second the words left my mouth, I wished I could swallow them back.

Ava's face changed.

Like a door inside her clicked shut.

"Oh," she said. "Okay."

"No, I didn't mean it like that."

"Sure."

"No, really. I'm serious."

"Then say something serious."

I opened my mouth but nothing came out.

What was I supposed to say?

Sorry I called you exhausting in front of the entire school and at least three teachers?

Sorry I made it sound like you play the victim because I was annoyed and jealous and wanted Becca to agree with me for thirty seconds?

Sorry I turned whatever was going on with you into entertainment?

Ava looked away first.

That made me feel worse than if she'd kept staring.

"You know what the funniest part is?" she said.

I didn't answer. I was pretty sure there was no funny part.

"I wasn't even upset about what people were saying yesterday. Not really." She let out a short breath through her nose. "I'm used to rumors. I was upset because Jayden was trying to shut it down and people kept making it worse."

My stomach dropped.

"Oh."

"Yeah. Oh."

The bus turned onto our street then, big and yellow and horrifyingly on schedule.

Ava stepped back. "See you at school, Mia."

She got on without looking at me again.

I climbed on after her, my legs weirdly shaky, and knew before I even reached the aisle that everybody had already chosen this as the most interesting thing that had ever happened to them.

Heads turned.

There was whispering. People suddenly checking their phones. Then silence. Noticeably so. Painfully so.

Becca waved frantically from halfway down the bus. I slid in next to her.

"Oh my gosh," she whispered the second I sat down. "You talked to her?"

"Kind of."

Her eyes widened. "And? What did she say?"

"She totally hates me."

"She doesn't hate you."

I met her eyes.

"Okay, she might hate you a little right now," Becca said. "Can you really blame her?"

"Helpful."

"I'm being honest."

"That's not the same thing."

She tucked a piece of hair behind her ear and lowered her voice even more. "You need to be ready."

"For what?"

"For everybody."

As if summoned by the word, Ryder twisted around from the seat in front of us. "Yo, Mia."

"Don't," I said.

He grinned. "I was just gonna ask if you're planning any more school-wide announcements today."

Becca kicked the back of his seat. "Turn around, loser."

He laughed and did, which was lucky for him. I was not in the mood.

I watched the houses blur by in the cold morning light and tried not to think.

That lasted about eight seconds.

By the time we got to school, my phone had three new texts from people I barely talked to and one message request from somebody in ninth grade, which felt deeply unfair.

The hallway was loud in that normal morning way—lockers slamming, sneakers squeaking, too much perfume, too many voices—

but underneath it ran a different kind of energy. One I could feel turning as I walked by.

Not everyone looked at me.

Just most. Casually, trying not to be caught doing it.

I saw it in pieces.

A pause in conversation.

A glance.

A quick whisper.

A smirk.

Becca stayed glued to my side like a witness protection volunteer as we moved toward the office.

"At least get the office part over with first," she said. "Maybe after that you'll feel better."

I stopped walking. "That's not how this works."

She sighed. "Sorry. Just trying to help."

"I can tell."

Which was true. She was trying. She was also the kind of person who found all social disasters a little interesting, even when they belonged to her friends.

At the front office door, she squeezed my arm. "Text me after. Let me know how it goes."

"As if I'm ever texting again."

"That seems like an overreaction."

I gave her a flat look.

She winced. "Or not."

Inside, everything smelled like printer paper and lemon cleaner.

The secretary looked up. "Mia? Mr. Harlow is expecting you."

No kidding.

Assistant Principal Harlow's door was open. He stood beside his desk in a tie too bright and cheerful for the circumstances, holding a travel mug and reading something on his computer.

Probably my 'social' death certificate.

He looked up and gave me a smile that was trying very hard to be Mr. Calm Adult and not Mr. Disappointed Authority Figure.

"Mia. Come on in."

I stepped inside and sat in the chair across from his desk.

He closed the door.

Mr. Harlow was the type of adult who liked to point out your mistakes, and he never seemed short of excuses to get a student into his office.

I thought I was prepared for his face. I was wrong. The sound of the door closing shaved about five years off my life. I was already fighting back tears and the real conversation hadn't even started.

He didn't say anything at first. He sat down, folded his hands, and looked at me the way adults do when they want you to feel the weight of your own choices before they start talking.

It worked.

"Do you understand why I asked you to come in this morning?" he said.

I gave a nod.

"Use your words, please."

"Yes," I muttered. "Because of the group chat."

"Because of the message you sent in the group chat," he corrected gently.

Another thing he always did—if you weren't exact, he'd jump in and fix it for you. It felt like a small kind of bullying.

My ears burned. "Yes."

He glanced down at a printed sheet on his desk.

Printed. He'd actually printed it. There is no humiliation like watching your worst decision become office paperwork.

"Can you explain to me what happened?"

There were at least three ways to answer that.

The easy way.

The technical way.

The honest way.

A crack in the corner of his desk suddenly became fascinating, and I picked the middle one.

"It was a total accident. I meant to send it only to my friend Becca. Somehow, I sent it to the community chat instead."

Mr. Harlow nodded once. "All right."

He waited. He was waiting for more.

"I was upset," I added. "And I wasn't thinking."

"That part is clear."

I lifted my gaze. I'd hoped he'd cut me some slack, since it was an accident. He didn't sound like he had any to spare.

His tone wasn't mean exactly. Just sharp.

He slid the paper a little closer to himself. "Mia, whether you intended to send it to the larger group or not, you named specific students, made negative personal comments, and added to an ongoing rumor."

My gaze dropped to my knees. "I am aware."

"Are you?"

That stung. Tears filled my eyes and I blinked fast to fight them off. Then I nodded anyway.

He leaned back. "Here's the problem. When things are written and sent publicly, they take on a different weight. Even if the original intention was private, the impact is now public. Do you understand the difference?"

"Yes." It came out smaller than I meant.

He was quiet a moment. Then he said, "Ava was in here this morning too."

My head snapped up. "She was?"

"Yes."

My stomach clenched. "Is she in trouble?"

"No."

I was relieved. None of this was her fault.

"At this point," he continued, "I'm less interested in punishment than in how you plan to fix the damage."

The word damage sat between us heavily.

I had embarrassed her. That much was already clear. But damage sounded bigger. More permanent.

"So, what happens now?" I asked.

He folded his hands again. "You'll be staying in during lunch today. We'll also be contacting your parents. And I expect you to give serious thought to an apology."

An apology. That word should have felt obvious. Instead it made panic flare all over again.

Apologizing to Ava privately was one thing. That would be hard enough. Apologizing after the entire school had read what I wrote felt like trying to patch a window after the whole house had already flooded.

Mr. Harlow must have seen something on my face, because his expression softened.

"I'm not asking for a perfect speech," he said. "I'm just asking you to take some accountability."

I gave a nod. Then nodded again, because once hadn't felt like enough.

He let out a breath. "All right. Go to class. Keep your phone put away. And Mia?"

"Yeah?"

"Don't let the next decision be worse than the first one."

My throat tightened. "Okay."

When I left the office, the hallway seemed louder than before. Or maybe I'd just lost the ability to separate noise from panic.

Becca spotted me from across the lockers and hurried over. "Well?"

"They're calling my mom."

She winced. "Oh man."

"I have lunch detention."

"That's not so bad."

I met her eyes.

She held up both hands. "Not saying it's good. Just saying you're not expelled."

"Thanks for the optimism."

"You're welcome." She lowered her voice. "Did he say anything about Ava?"

I shifted my backpack higher. "She was already in there."

Becca's eyes widened. "Before you?"

I gave a nod.

"Dang."

"Can you not say dang like this is a podcast recap?"

She pressed her lips together. "Sorry."

We started toward first period. Halfway down the hall, I saw Jayden.

He was by the drinking fountain with two other boys from his soccer group, one foot against the wall, talking with his hands the way he always did when he got animated. For a second he looked like normal Jayden. Funny Jayden. Easy Jayden. The version everybody liked.

He saw me and stopped smiling. He'd read the message. It was like a light had been turned down behind his face.

His friends noticed too. One went quiet. The other suddenly found the floor fascinating.

I should have kept walking. Instead, I slowed.

Jayden pushed away from the wall. "Mia."

Just my name. But it made Becca tense beside me.

"Hi," I said, since I seemed committed to sounding useless in every interaction for the rest of my life.

He held my gaze a moment. "Can I talk to you later?"

I nodded before I could think better of it. "Sure."

He looked like he might say something else. Then the warning bell rang, slicing through the hallway.

Everybody started moving again.

Jayden stepped back. "Later, then." He headed off toward his class.

Becca turned to me the second he was out of earshot. "Oh my gosh."

"Please do not."

"He wants to talk to you."

"Yes, I heard him."

"Do you think he's mad?"

I gave her a look.

She considered. "Okay, yes, obviously. But like regular mad or secretly hurt mad?"

"Why would that help me?"

"It wouldn't. I'm just wondering."

That was Becca in one sentence. She loved the juicy details as much as anyone.

We reached first period just before the late bell. I slid into my seat, pulled out my notebook, and spent the first ten minutes pretending to copy the warm-up while my brain replayed every second of the morning on a loop.

Ava's face in the driveway.

Mr. Harlow saying things.

Jayden asking to talk later.

My mom getting a call.

The entire school knowing.

And under all of it, one thought I still couldn't shake:

What if Ava was right?

What if I really had said all of it like I knew something, when I knew almost nothing?

I looked across the room. Ava was two rows over by the windows.

She didn't look at me once.

That, more than anything, made my chest feel tight.

Anger I could have handled. Yelling, even. Silence was harder. Silence meant the space between us had changed shape overnight.

And it was my fault.

When the teacher turned to write on the board, Ryder leaned sideways in the seat ahead of me and whispered, "Tough crowd today, huh?"

I kicked the leg of his chair. A second later, I wished I'd aimed higher. Not too hard. Just enough to save him from himself.

He grinned forward again.

I looked down at my notebook and wrote the date three times before I realized I wasn't listening to anything.

This day was not even one class old.

And already it felt too long to survive.

Humiliation

Ava:

I was already having a bad day when Mia's message hit the eighth-grade chat.

Not like the movie type of bad day where somebody dumps a milkshake on your head or you fail a test you forgot to study for.

Just the stressful kind.

The kind where your name keeps coming up from random places, and every time somebody looks at you, you have to figure out whether they know something, think they know something, or are about to ask about something. Exhausting.

By lunch, Tessa had heard that I was crying in the bathroom.

By sixth period, Lila heard it was Jayden who made me cry.

By the end of the day, somebody else had decided Jayden and I had been secretly texting for weeks and were more than just friends. This would have been impressive considering none of that had actually happened.

Rumors at school never arrived as one complete lie. They showed up in pieces. A comment here. A screenshot there. Somebody swearing they had the real story this time. By the end, the original version barely mattered because people liked the pieced together, made up one more.

I was at my locker after last bell when Tessa came over holding her phone in front of her like it contained state secrets.

"You need to see this," she said.

"I really don't."

"No, seriously."

Lila was right behind her, already wearing the exact face people wear when something is either deeply embarrassing or deeply entertaining and they have not decided which yet.

Tessa turned the phone toward me.

It was a screenshot from one of those fake anonymous accounts people made whenever they got bored and needed to ruin somebody else's week.

The post said: ***heard ava s and jayden r have been acting like they arent together but literally everyone knows***

Underneath that, someone had commented:

wait i thought she liked someone else

Someone else:

shes been crying all day lol

I read it. Then once more.

My whole body went hot and cold at the same time.

"This is so dumb," I said, which would have sounded more convincing if my voice hadn't gone thin.

Tessa lowered the phone a little. "It sure is."

"People are actually insane."

Lila shifted her backpack higher on her shoulder. "It's probably just somebody being weird."

That was not helpful enough to count as helpful.

I looked away from the screen and shut my locker harder than I meant to. "Can they not use my life as a group project for like five minutes?"

Tessa gave me a look that was mostly sympathy and a little alarm. "Do you want me to report the account?"

"To who? Would it even make a difference?"

"I'm serious."

"So am I."

I started walking toward the side doors before either of them could say anything else.

They followed, of course.

I wasn't crying.

That part matters. To me at least.

People always say crying when what they really mean is looked upset in public, and it appears that we have all agreed as a society that girls are only allowed two emotions: fine or crying.

I was not crying but I was furious.

And embarrassed. Which I wish I wasn't.

It was one thing for random people to invent some fake thing about me and Jayden. It was another thing knowing half the school was now watching my face to see if I reacted in a way that proved it.

As soon as I got outside, I saw Jayden near the bike rack with two boys from soccer.

He noticed me right away.

That was the thing with Jayden. He noticed people. He was good at it.

He said something to the boys, then jogged over before I could pretend not to see him.

"Hey," he said. "How you doing?"

Not, are the rumors true. Not, what happened. Just that.

It made everything in my chest feel tighter.

"Fine," I muttered.

He gave me a look.

It was not an accusing look. Just accurate.

"Okay," he said. "You seem extremely fine."

Despite everything, I almost smiled.

Almost.

"People are being dumb," I said.

He nodded. "Yeah. I saw."

He had. Obviously.

If my name was in it, his was too.

I crossed my arms. "Sorry."

"For what?"

"For you getting dragged into all this drama."

Jayden shrugged one shoulder. "I'm less worried about me."

That did not help nearly as much as he probably meant it to.

Tessa and Lila hovered a little way off, trying to look casual and failing so badly it was embarrassing for all of us.

Jayden glanced at them, then back at me. "Do you want me to say something?"

I blinked once. "Like what?"

"I don't know. That it's not true?"

The weird thing was, he sounded like he actually meant it. Like he would have posted something right then if I said yes.

And maybe that should have made me feel better.

Instead, it made me feel exhausted.

The second a boy steps in to fix something, people act like that proves there was something to fix.

"No," I said. "That'll just make it worse."

He tilted his head a little. "Probably."

That was one thing I liked about Jayden. He almost never tried to pretend things were less awkward than they were.

He shoved his hands into his hoodie pocket. "For what it's worth, the whole thing is dumb."

I breathed out through my nose. "That's not worth a whole lot, but thanks."

That got a small laugh out of him.

He nodded once. "See you tomorrow?"

There was something so normal about that question I could have hugged him for it.

Instead, I just said, "Yeah."

"I'm around if I can help."

He headed off, and I stood there feeling weirdly suspended, like the day had been bad but at least it had not become a full disaster yet.

My phone buzzed.

I thought maybe it would be Tessa, even though she was standing ten feet away.

It was not.

It was our school's group chat - PANTHER PRIDE 8TH GRADE COMMUNITY.

Usually that only meant some teacher reminding us about forms or spirit week or needing volunteers for something nobody wanted to do.

I opened it without thinking.

Right there.

k im sry but ava is seriously exhausting

every week its some new drama but somehow everyones supposed to feel bad for her

and now jaydens involved too and honestly im not even surprised

if they want attention that bad then just say that

I genuinely did not understand what I was looking at.

I saw the name above them.

Mia Saunders

Everything inside me went still.

Tessa made a noise beside me. "Oh my gosh."

Lila actually said, "No way," under her breath like she was watching a live crash she could not believe had happened in front of her.

The screen glowed back at me.

Mia.

Not some random girl I barely knew.

Not somebody from another lunch table who thought they were funny.

Mia.

My neighbor.

The person whose mom still sent over Christmas cookies in a snowman tin.

The person who used to sit cross-legged on my bedroom floor in elementary school and rank all the boys in our class by who looked most likely to eat glue or pick their nose and eat it.

The person who knew exactly where I lived, where my room was, what my dog's name had been before he died, which fence board in our backyard came loose if you kicked it hard enough.

Mia.

It is strange how fast humiliation can turn into something harder.

I didn't even feel my face change.

But suddenly the fake account did not matter.

The rumor did not matter.

None of the dumb comments mattered as much as the fact that Mia had thought that.

And had written it down.

And had posted it where everyone could see.

Jayden's phone buzzed too.

I saw him glance down at it from across the lot then look up.

Straight at me.

I turned away first.

Totally embarrassed.

Not at the message itself at the audience.

The instant understanding that everybody connected to it now had front-row seats to my humiliation.

More notifications started dropping into the chat.

Ryder: wait WHAT

Another message came in.

Sophie: mia omg

Then:

Derek: yoooo

Tessa reached for my arm. "Ava—"

I pulled away without meaning to.

Not from her. From the whole moment. From all of it.

"I need to get out of here," I said.

Lila frowned. "Do you want us to walk with you?"

"No."

It came out too sharp.

Both of them went quiet.

I felt bad instantly, but not bad enough to fix it.

I started down the sidewalk without another word, my phone buzzing every few seconds in my hand.

One message after another.

Some direct. Some in the community chat. Some from people I had not talked to in weeks suddenly deciding now was the time to check in, which was insulting.

I did not open most of them.

I opened Mia's again.

I hated myself that much.

ava is seriously exhausting

That part sat there hitting me like I was a punching bag.

Exhausting.

That was not random-girl language.

That was the kind of word someone uses when they have been collecting irritation for a while.

By the time I got to my driveway, I was shaking in that furious, humiliated way where your body feels like it is trying to peel itself inside out.

My mom was in the front garden trimming back dead stems from last year and looked up when she saw me.

"You're home early."

I met her eyes.

At the shears in her hand.

Back at her.

And that was what almost did it.

The fact that my mom was standing there in old gardening gloves, looking normal, while my social life was disintegrating in real time.

"I'm going inside," I said.

She straightened. "Everything okay?"

"No, but I'll get through it."

That answer surprised both of us.

She followed me in.

I kicked off my shoes in the entryway and headed straight to the kitchen because for some reason standing in the middle of the room felt easier than sitting.

My mom set the shears on the counter. "Ava."

I handed her my phone.

That was all I had energy for.

She read the text.

Read it again.

Her mouth tightened in that dangerous adult way where they are trying not to react too fast.

"Who sent this?"

I met her eyes.

She looked up. "Right. Dumb question."

"Mom."

"Alright."

She handed the phone back carefully, like it might be hot.

"How many people are in that chat?"

"It's for the entire eighth grade. Teachers. Staff. Everybody."

She closed her eyes for one second. "Wow."

I sat down at the table before my legs could decide otherwise.

My mom pulled out the chair across from me. "Do you want me to call her mom?"

"No."

The answer came instantly.

Too instantly, probably.

"Okay," she said.

"I mean it."

"I heard you."

"I don't want this to turn into moms talking over the fence."

That almost made her smile, but not quite.

"That's fair."

My gaze dropped to the table.

For a while neither of us said anything.

She asked, "Is any of it true?"

I laughed once, but there was nothing funny in it.

"No."

"Nothing?"

"Nothing."

My mom nodded slowly. "Then I'm sorry."

The thing I had not even fully let myself feel yet.

Not just embarrassment.

Not just anger.

The ugly unfairness of being turned into a story that wasn't true, then watching someone who actually knew you help spread it anyway.

"Why would she even say that?" I asked.

My mom did not answer right away.

She was smart enough to know I was not really asking for a theory.

"I don't know," she said finally.

That made me angrier than any fake explanation would have.

My phone buzzed again.

A message from Mia.

I left it unopened for as long as I could stand.

My mom saw my face. "What?"

"She texted me."

"Do you want to read it?"

"No."

I did anyway.

ava im so sorry i didnt mean to post that in the group chat

The words blurred in front of me.

Not i didnt mean that.

Not i was wrong.

Just i didnt mean to post that

The location of the knife was the problem. I had been stabbed in the back and the knife was stuck there for all to see.

I locked my phone.

My mom didn't ask what it said.

Thankfully.

If I had read it out loud, I might have thrown something.

That night, I barely touched dinner.

Tessa texted three times. Lila twice. Sophie once, which I ignored on principle. Jayden sent one message that just said:

you okay

I let it sit there for a long time before writing back: not really

He replied almost right away:

yeah

That was all.

And weirdly, that helped more than I wanted it to.

At least it sounded honest.

Later, when I was brushing my teeth, I saw movement through the bathroom window.

Across the yards, through the dark, Mia's bedroom light was still on.

I stood there with toothpaste foam in my mouth, watching the square of yellow light like it might explain something if I looked long enough.

It didn't.

If I could throw a rock and hit her window right now, would it make me feel better?

Probably not.

The next morning, I was at the end of my driveway with Tessa and Lila when Mia came out of her house.

Tessa was saying something about science homework.

Lila was laughing.

Mia appeared, and both of them went quiet so fast it was almost funny.

Mia looked awful.

I don't say that to be mean.

She looked as if she'd barely-slept, in a fully-panicked way.

For one second, I saw the version of her I had known forever.

The girl who once cried because she thought she had killed her goldfish by overfeeding it, even though it turned out the fish had just been really old.

The girl who used to borrow my markers and forget to put the caps back on.

The girl who always got too intense too fast when she was upset.

I remembered the message.

That version disappeared.

She walked toward us, not fast, not slow, just trapped by the fact that there was only one sidewalk and she had to use it.

When she got close enough, I said her name.

"Mia."

She stopped.

"Hey," she said.

Hey.

That almost made me laugh.

Like we were about to discuss borrowed homework instead of the fact that she had detonated my week in front of the entire grade.

"So," I said.

She swallowed.

I could see how hard she was trying to come up with the right words.

That would have mattered more if I had not spent half the night staring at the wrong ones.

"Were you going to talk to me," I asked, "or were you waiting for the office to do it first?"

That had some effect.

Good.

Not so deep down, a mean part of me wanted it to.

She said she had been going to talk to me.

I didn't believe her.

Not fully.

Maybe that was unfair.

Then again, so was the group chat.

I told her what I actually cared about.

Not that she had vented to Becca. That still hurt, but it was not the deepest cut.

The deepest cut was how certain she had sounded.

Like she knew me.

Like she knew what I was doing.

Like she had been saving up reasons.

"You could've just asked me," I said.

She said she knew.

And maybe she did.

She said, "What do you want me to say?"

That was the moment something in me snapped colder.

There it was, the piece underneath the apology.

The irritation. The defensiveness. The tiny suggestion that maybe I was making this harder than it had to be.

I stepped back before I said something I could not take back.

The bus turned the corner right then, loud and yellow and exactly on time, because the universe enjoys dramatic timing more than the rest of us.

I got on without looking at her again.

Tessa slid over in the seat to make room for me.

"What happened?" she whispered.

I looked out the window as Mia climbed onto the bus behind us.

"Nothing," I said.

That was not true.

But it was the only answer I had.

The real truth was bigger and messier than one conversation on a sidewalk.

The real truth was that Mia and I had not been fine for a while.

This just happened to be the first time everybody else got to see it.

Under the Microscope

Mia:

Somewhere in last period, I worked out a new theory about school.

It was not designed for learning.

It was designed to see how long a person could survive under low-grade humiliation before doing something medically interesting.

All day, I had been looked at just enough to make me paranoid.

Not enough to let me get used to it.

Just enough.

A pause when I walked into class.

A whisper that stopped half a second too late.

Someone glancing up from their phone and then pretending they had not just been reading about me.

By seventh period, even the teachers seemed weird.

Not openly weird. Subtle weird.

The kind where they were either trying too hard to act normal or watching me with that careful adult expression that meant they knew everything and were waiting to see if I would make it worse.

Which, to be fair, felt like a reasonable concern.

I shoved books into my backpack harder than necessary and tried not to look across the room at Ava.

She was laughing at something Tessa said.

Actually laughing.

That should not have bothered me.

It absolutely did.

And that last possibility felt the worst.

Becca slid up next to my desk as the room emptied. "So."

I met her eyes. "If you say so one more time, I'm transferring to another school in another state and you'll never see me again."

She ignored that. "Have you thought about what you're going to do?"

"Yes."

"And?"

"I've thought about how I'd like to move to another state."

"That's not a realistic plan."

"It's an emotionally realistic plan."

Becca hitched her backpack higher. "I'm serious, Mia."

"I know."

We stepped into the hallway with everyone else, carried forward in that loud after-school river of bodies and backpacks and people pretending not to care what everyone else was doing.

Which, in middle school, was the national sport.

Becca lowered her voice. "Did you talk to Ava again?"

"No."

"Jayden?"

I gave her a look.

That answered enough.

Her eyebrows went up. "Oh my gosh."

"Please stop reacting like I'm a reality show."

"I'm not," she said. "I'm reacting like you're my best friend and this is a lot."

That made me feel bad. She wasn't wrong.

I slowed at my locker and spun the combination too fast the first time. Then too slow the second.

Becca leaned against the one next to mine. "Okay. So, what happened?"

I pulled open the locker and stared at the pile of books inside like they had answers.

"He knows."

Becca blinked. "Knows what?"

I met her eyes.

Her eyes widened. "Oh."

"Exactly."

"How?"

"I'm not even fully sure. He just—figured it out."

She pressed both hands over her mouth, which was not supportive but was at least honest.

"I hate you," I muttered.

"You do not."

"I do right now."

Becca dropped her hands. "Did he make it weird?"

I shoved a notebook into my bag. "Everything is weird."

"That's not what I asked."

I sighed. "No. Not exactly."

She studied my face. "Okay. So worse?"

"It somehow is."

"With a lunch detention, a probably-upcoming parental disaster, Ava hating me, and Jayden now knowing I'm a complete idiot."

"That is one version."

"It is the correct version."

Becca folded her arms. "What about the rumor?"

I stopped moving.

That was the real problem sitting under all the other problems.

The rumor.

Still out there. Still moving. Still attached to Ava and Jayden whether they wanted it or not.

And now, thanks to me, probably moving faster.

I shut my locker. "What about it?"

Becca frowned. "Are people still talking?"

I gave her a flat look.

She considered. "Right. Dumb question."

A group of seventh graders passed us, and one of them looked at me, whispered something to the others, and immediately looked away.

I wanted to evaporate.

"I don't know what I'm supposed to do," I said quietly.

Becca's expression shifted a little. Less fascinated. More real.

"Did you apologize?"

"I did."

"To Ava?"

"Kind of."

Becca tilted her head. "Kind of is not a word people use when the apology went well."

"It did not go well."

"Mia."

"I know."

"No, I mean really. You can't just say sorry and then act annoyed she didn't instantly forgive you."

I met her eyes.

"That is unfortunately wise," I admitted.

"I have my moments."

She glanced down the hall, then back at me. "You might have to say something more meaningful."

I knew exactly what she meant.

And I hated it on sight.

"No."

Becca winced. "You didn't even let me finish."

"You were going to say I should put something in the chat."

"Maybe."

"No."

"Mia—"

"No. Absolutely not."

Saying something publicly meant reopening it publicly.

It meant dragging my own humiliation back into the light and handing everyone a second round.

It meant screenshottable remorse.

Permanent evidence of me being wrong in two directions instead of one.

I started walking toward the front doors before Becca could keep going.

She hurried after me. "Okay, but listen."

"I am listening against my will."

"If people still think Ava and Jayden are a thing, and they only think that because you helped make it bigger—"

"I am aware."

"Then staying quiet now is also a choice."

That stopped me.

We reached the front entrance just as a rush of students pushed outside, voices spilling into the cold air.

I spotted Jayden near the bike rack again.

That area had become his natural habitat.

He was with Ryder and another boy from soccer, laughing at something, and for one dangerous second everything looked normal enough that my brain tried to forget the last twenty-four hours.

Ryder noticed me.

Obviously, he did.

Ryder was the kind of person who could detect possible awkwardness the way sharks detect blood in water.

He elbowed Jayden once and said something I could not hear.

Jayden looked over.

I turned away immediately, which was mature and cool.

"Mia," Becca said.

"I know he exists."

"That is not what I was going to say."

"Then what?"

"Ava."

I turned.

Ava was coming down the front steps with Tessa and Lila, all three of them in a cluster that looked casual from far away and impossible to approach up close.

For one second, all the paths lined up wrong.

Me by the bike rack.

Jayden already there.

Ava headed straight toward the same sidewalk exit.

It felt like the universe had arranged a group project in suffering.

"Great," I muttered.

Becca made a tiny sound under her breath. "Maybe this is good?"

"There is genuinely something wrong with your brain."

But nobody got the chance to collide.

Just then, a boy from eighth-grade homeroom—Derek, I think—said loudly to nobody and everybody, "Yo, are y'all dating or not?"

The whole area did not go silent exactly.

It did something worse.

It thinned.

Like the noise stepped back to make room.

Jayden's face changed instantly.

Not embarrassed.

Annoyed.

Ava stopped walking.

Tessa muttered, "Oh my gosh."

My own stomach dropped somewhere near the sidewalk.

Derek laughed like he had just done something hilarious instead of socially setting the building on fire.

Jayden looked at him. "What?"

Derek shrugged, still grinning. "I'm just asking, man. Everybody's saying stuff."

Ava folded her arms.

Not dramatic.

More like defensive or even protective.

Like she had been forced back into the middle of something she had not asked for.

The only thing I could think was this was still happening because of me.

Even if Derek had already heard the rumor before, my text had put it in neon. My message had taken a mutter and turned it into a spotlight.

Jayden took one step toward Derek. "Then everybody should get better hobbies."

A couple of kids laughed nervously.

Derek held up both hands. "Dang, okay."

Ava looked down, then away, like she was trying very hard not to react in public.

It made me feel for her.

Suddenly I could see it from the outside.

What Ava had meant this morning.

How exhausting it must be to feel a whole crowd waiting to see what your face does.

Tessa touched Ava's sleeve. "Come on."

They started walking again.

And before I could stop myself—before I could think better of it, which seemed to be my lifelong pattern—I stepped forward.

"Derek," I said.

My voice was not loud.

It did not need to be.

He turned.

So did half the people near him.

My pulse slammed against my ribs.

Becca made a tiny panicked noise beside me.

"What?" Derek said.

I could still back out.

I should have backed out.

Instead, I heard myself say, "It's not true."

Nobody moved.

Derek blinked. "What?"

"The rumor," I said, louder this time because public self-destruction had become a skill set. "About Ava and Jayden. It's not true."

A few people looked at each other.

Someone shifted a backpack.

Ryder's eyebrows went up.

Jayden stared at me.

Ava had stopped walking again.

I could feel her attention like heat on the side of my face.

Derek shrugged. "Okay?"

That should have been the end of it.

It wasn't.

The thing about finally saying one true thing out loud is that it tends to drag the next one right behind it.

"And I made it worse," I said.

Becca whispered, "Mia."

I kept going anyway.

"I heard stuff that wasn't true, and I repeated it, and I shouldn't have."

The silence around us deepened.

I was dimly aware that this was maybe the most horrifying moment of my life.

They were watching.

Actually watching.

No jokes. No whispers. Just attention.

Derek's grin had disappeared.

This time, he looked less like entertainment and more like somebody realizing a real person had entered the conversation.

Ava still hadn't said anything.

Neither had Jayden.

I could feel my face burning all the way to my ears.

"Okay," Derek said finally, a lot quieter.

It was not an apology.

But it was also not another joke.

Which, from him, practically counted as growth.

I turned to Ava then.

Not dramatically. Just because I couldn't not look at her.

Her expression was impossible to read.

Not soft.

Just surprised.

Which, honestly was totally fair.

Tessa looked between us like she had accidentally walked into a scene she was not prepared to understand.

Lila had gone fully motionless.

Jayden's face had changed too.

Not amused. Not triumphant.

Almost concerned.

As if he was realizing I had chosen public honesty and might not survive it.

Which, to be fair, was a possibility.

My throat tightened. "So maybe people should stop saying it."

Nobody answered.

A bus hissed at the curb.

A car door slammed somewhere in the lot.

And then, because the universe could not let a single social death be clean, Ryder said, "Yeah, maybe."

His words made me want to cry more than if he had just laughed.

The spell broke a little after that.

People moved again. Talked again. Not totally back to normal, but enough.

Derek muttered, "Whatever," and drifted off.

Jayden looked at Ava.

She gave the smallest nod.

He nodded back.

He glanced at me once, brief but unreadable, before heading toward the parking lot with Ryder.

That left me standing in the cold with Becca on one side and Ava ten feet away.

The distance between us felt absurdly specific.

Tessa and Lila looked at Ava.

Ava looked at me.

I had no idea what happened next.

Neither did anyone else.

Finally, Ava said, "That was."

There are moments when the right response appears in your mind too late to be useful.

I did not have that problem.

I had no response at all.

"Yeah," I said.

Excellent.

Ava adjusted the strap on her backpack. "I have to go."

"Okay."

She hesitated.

So briefly I might have imagined it.

She walked off with Tessa and Lila.

I stood there long enough for Becca to physically grab my sleeve.

"What," she said, "was that?"

I let out a breath that felt scraped out of me. "I don't know."

"You just made a public statement."

"In front of Derek. Which, I mean good for you."

Becca stared after Ava's group, then at Jayden disappearing across the lot. "That was not nothing."

"I know."

"How do you feel?"

I considered it.

Like I had walked straight into traffic, mostly.

But also—

A tiny bit less trapped.

Which was annoying.

"Terrible," I said.

Becca nodded. "Makes sense."

We started toward the buses.

Halfway there, my phone buzzed.

My gaze dropped.

A message from my mom.

Got a call from school. We need to talk about this.

We did. Naturally.

I locked my phone without answering.

Becca saw my face. "Parents?"

"Yes."

She hissed in sympathy. "Oof."

We climbed onto the bus, and for once nobody said anything to me.

That should have felt like relief.

Instead, it felt like waiting.

Like whatever happened in the parking lot had not ended anything. It had just moved the pieces.

I slid into a seat by the window and watched the school shrink behind us.

Across the aisle, two girls were whispering over a phone.

Three rows up, Ryder said something to Jayden that made Jayden shake his head.

Toward the front, Ava sat with Tessa, staring straight ahead.

I rested my forehead against the cold glass.

The problem with finally doing the right thing, I was starting to realize, was that it did not erase the wrong thing.

It just meant you had to live with both.

And tonight, I still had to tell my mom everything.

Consequences

Mia Continued:

Somewhere between the bus and my front door, I developed a deep respect for people who live alone in the woods without cell phones.

I wanted that life.

Not forever, probably.

Just until everybody at school forgot I existed.

The bus ride home had been weirdly quiet. Not normal quiet. The kind where people had definitely already used up most of their gossip energy during the day and were now saving the rest for dinner tables, bedroom group chats, and whatever horrifying after-school version of social analysis eighth graders turned into once they got home and had snacks.

I got off at my stop with Becca, and we just stood there on the sidewalk like neither of us was sure what came next.

"You should probably text me later," she said.

I met her eyes.

"Or not," she added. "That was obviously the wrong verb choice."

"Yes. It was."

Becca winced. "Sorry."

That word meant less to me lately.

It was everywhere now. Sorry from me, sorry from Becca, sorry from teachers in the form of concerned eyebrows, sorry from adults who said things like *learning opportunity* while your life actively collapsed in front of them.

I adjusted my backpack. "I'll talk to you later."

"That sounds worse."

"It probably is."

She shoved her hands into her hoodie pocket. "Mia."

I stopped.

She looked like she wanted to say something helpful and was realizing in real time that helpful had left the building three disasters ago.

"I didn't think you'd actually send it there," she said finally.

I met her eyes.

She immediately grimaced. "Wow. Horrible sentence. I know that."

"You think?"

"I mean—I know you know that." She pressed her lips together. "I just mean I didn't think… I don't know. I didn't think it would blow up like this."

That made something ugly twist in my chest.

Neither did I.

And maybe that was part of what was so terrible. Not just that I'd done it. That some part of me had sent those words into the world without really thinking of them as dangerous.

Like words didn't count unless you meant for them to be heard by all.

Like cruelty only mattered by audience size.

"I have to go," I said.

Becca nodded. "Okay."

I started walking.

"Mia?"

I turned back again, since this had become a day full of other people making me stop walking so they could say difficult things.

Becca looked smaller.

Not physically. Just less sure of herself.

"For what it's worth," she said, "I don't think you're a bad person."

That should have helped.

Instead, it made my throat feel weird.

Bad people probably didn't spend this much time wondering whether they were bad.

And good people probably did not accidentally humiliate their neighbors in front of an entire grade and multiple faculty members.

So, I was stuck living in the deeply uncomfortable middle.

"Thanks," I said.

I went home.

The second I walked through the front door, I knew my mom was waiting.

Not in a dramatic, sitting-in-the-dark way.

In the much scarier normal-parent way where she was standing at the kitchen counter pretending to wipe it down even though it was already clean.

She looked up when I came in.

I went still.

"I'm guessing," she said, "you know why I got a call from school."

There are moments when lying is technically possible but spiritually exhausting.

This was one of them.

"Yeah."

She set the rag down.

"Mia."

Not angry.

Just tired.

I dropped my backpack by the stairs. "Can we not do this the second I get home?"

Her eyebrows lifted. "That depends. Were you planning to explain it later in a way that would make it less true?"

I hated when she was good at this.

I kicked off my shoes and headed for the kitchen because public disaster was not enough and now, I also wanted private discomfort with snacks nearby.

My mom pulled out one of the chairs at the table and sat down. Not the position of a person who was about to let something go.

I sat too.

Neither of us said anything.

She slid her phone across the table.

On the screen was a screenshot of the message.

My message.

Still worse every time I saw it.

"How many people saw this?" she asked.

My gaze moved from the phone to the table.

"A lot."

"Mia."

"The whole grade. Teachers too."

She closed her eyes for one second like she was trying not to say the first ten things that came into her head.

When she opened them again, she looked calmer.

Which honestly felt threatening.

"Walk me through what happened."

I thought about doing the fast version.

The edited version.

The version where I looked like a person who had a very unlucky thumb and not a person who had typed four lines of real meanness and only felt immediate full regret once the audience got too large to survive.

Instead, I focused on a knot in the wood grain and said, "I heard a rumor. I got mad. I texted Becca. Or I meant to. And I sent it to the wrong chat."

My mom nodded once.

"Why were you mad?"

The answer should have been simple.

It wasn't.

"Because Ava was in the middle of everything again," I said.

"Again?"

I shrugged, which was a terrible response but I had already committed to being bad at this.

My mom watched me carefully. "That sounds like it didn't start yesterday."

My gaze dropped.

The issue underneath it.

The thing I had not wanted adults to see because once adults saw it, it became less of a social mistake and more of a character issue.

"No," I said quietly.

She leaned back slightly in her chair. "So, this wasn't just one bad text. This was one bad text sitting on top of older feelings."

I hated that sentence because it was accurate and sounded like something that should be embroidered on a pillow and handed back to me as evidence.

"I guess."

"You guess?"

"Yes," I said, more sharply than I meant to. "Okay? Yes."

My mom did not flinch.

She almost never did when I snapped. Which was annoying. It robbed me of the ability to feel dramatically misunderstood.

"Do you want to tell me what those older feelings are?" she asked.

No.

Absolutely not.

I wanted to tell her nothing.

I wanted to become one of those lizards that flattened itself under rocks when threatened. Or better yet, a turtle who could just close up her shell and hide.

Instead, I said, "Not really."

She nodded slowly. "Fair enough."

That surprised me enough that I lifted my gaze.

She folded her hands on the table. "I'm not going to force every part of this out of you tonight. But I am going to say a few things."

That sentence felt extremely mom-shaped and dangerous.

"First," she said, "whether you meant to send it publicly or not, you still wrote it."

My gaze dropped back to the table.

"Second, being embarrassed about being caught is not the same as being sorry for being cruel."

That one felt like a slap.

I almost winced as somewhere inside all the panic and humiliation and wanting to rewind time, I knew that was the real question.

Was I sorry I got caught?

Or sorry I said it?

And if I was honest, the answer had started as the first one.

Now it was something uglier and more mixed up than that.

"I know," I said.

"Do you?"

There was that question again.

Everybody in my life had formed a committee around whether I truly understood things.

"Yes," I muttered.

My mom let out a breath. "Third, this situation is not over just because the school handled it. You need to think about what accountability looks like."

The word made my shoulders tighten.

"Mr. Harlow already said that."

"I'm glad one of us got there first."

I almost smiled.

Almost. If I had, it wouldn't have turned out very good for me.

Instead, I said, "I apologized."

My mom tilted her head. "To Ava?"

"Kind of."

She gave me a look.

I sighed. "Yes, to Ava. But not in some amazing perfect way."

"Was it about the harm you caused, or about how bad you feel?"

I opened my mouth.

Closed it.

That answered enough.

My mom nodded once, not unkindly. "Then you probably know what the problem is."

I hated that too.

I really did.

We were quiet.

I asked, "Are you mad?"

She looked at me for a long moment.

"I'm disappointed," she said. "And I think you made a mean choice. But mad isn't the main thing."

That made me look up.

"The main thing," she said, "is that I know you well enough to think this can teach you something if you let it."

That was such a parent sentence I almost rolled my eyes on instinct.

But I didn't.

I knew what she was really saying.

That I had messed up.

That she believed I could be better than this.

Which was a lot heavier than just being grounded.

"Am I grounded?" I asked.

My mom actually smiled then. Since I was still myself enough to ask the dumbest practical question in the middle of an emotional reckoning.

"Yes," she said. "Phone use only for school and direct communication this week. No hanging out after school. No weekend plans until we revisit it."

I groaned.

She raised one eyebrow.

"Right," I muttered. "Fair."

"Also," she added, "you are not deleting this from your life by disappearing into your room."

That was exactly my plan, so it was rude of her to say it so fast.

"I wasn't going to do that." I countered.

"Mia."

"Okay, maybe a little."

She stood up and took the screenshot-covered phone off the table.

"Homework first. Then dinner. Then you can go think dramatically in your room."

"Wow. Generous."

"I am known for it."

I dragged myself upstairs with my backpack feeling approximately a thousand pounds heavier than it had this morning.

My room looked the same.

That was the deal with disaster.

Your lamp still sat on your dresser. Your sweatshirt still hung over your chair. The half-read book on your nightstand still waited there like any of this mattered less than chapter twelve.

I dropped my backpack on the floor and took out my homework, which I stared at for a full minute before admitting to myself that molecules and vocabulary definitions were not happening until I got one thing out of my system.

I grabbed my phone.

Opened my messages.

Stared at the blank text box under Ava's name.

Typed:

im sorry

Too small.

Delete it.

im really sorry for what i said

Better.

Not good enough.

Deleted.

i know saying sorry doesnt fix it

Nah, too obvious.

Delete.

I tossed the phone onto my bed and flopped backward beside it.

The ceiling stared down at me with all the empathy of drywall.

After a minute, I sat back up and tried the group chat instead.

I guess part of me still liked dangerous ideas.

I opened PANTHER PRIDE 8TH GRADE COMMUNITY and immediately felt my stomach tighten.

Nothing in there had to do with me now.

Just normal school messages.

All that space. All that boring official normality. And right in the middle of its recent history, my disaster.

I tapped the message box.

Typed:

what i said about ava and jayden wasnt true

I went still.

Added:

i heard a rumor and repeated it and i made things worse

That part felt more real.

Then:

im sorry

I read the three lines about six times.

My thumb hovered over send.

The problem was, all of it was true.

The bigger problem was, true did not mean enough.

If I sent it, people would screenshot it.

Talk about it again.

Maybe believe it. Maybe mock it. Maybe decide I was only apologizing due to parents or teachers forced me to.

Maybe they'd be right.

I deleted the whole thing.

I started over.

Deleted it again.

By the third version, I wanted to throw my phone into the ocean.

A knock hit my half-open door.

I lifted my gaze.

My mom leaned against the frame. "Homework?"

I held up the worksheet like evidence of a tragic and ongoing battle.

She nodded toward my phone. "And?"

"I'm trying."

"That's good."

"It feels awful."

She gave me a sympathetic half-smile. "Also good."

"Not what I meant."

"I know."

She lingered a second. "You don't have to figure out the perfect version tonight."

That should have relieved me.

Instead, it made me want to cry a little, which was silly and unhelpful.

"I know."

She left.

I looked back at my phone.

At Ava's name.

At the group chat.

At Becca's.

I opened Becca first.

I went with the second-best choice first.

did u tell anyone else what i said before i sent it

The typing bubbles came almost immediately.

what do you mean

That took a second to process.

Typed:

becca

Long pause.

Then:

not like on purpose

That made something in my stomach drop.

I sat up straighter.

what does that mean

Another pause.

Longer this time.

Then:

i told taylor some of it at lunch before everything happened but not like the exact wording

The screen glowed back at me.

A hot wave of irritation rose in my chest.

Taylor knew.

By lunch, it had already been halfway around the grade in some blurry retold version.

My private anger had not even been fully private before I blew it up myself.

I typed:

you said not to worry earlier

She answered:

i meant not to worry before you accidentally detonated the school

I actually laughed once at that.

A horrible tiny laugh.

Because it was Becca and since she was trying and was perhaps a good part of why everything in middle school always became everybody's business.

Another message came through.

im sorry okay

i shouldnt have repeated it

I read those twice.

Locked my phone and dropped it beside me.

The thing under the thing under the thing.

Rumors did not just appear.

They got carried.

One person to the next. One private text to one lunch table to one fake account to one public mess.

And somewhere inside all of that, I had still chosen my part.

Later, after homework and a very quiet dinner and an extremely fake attempt to care about a history worksheet, I lay on my bed with my lamp on low and my phone in my hand again.

This time I opened Ava's messages and typed:

i know ur probably tired of hearing from me but i just wanted to say im sorry again and also im not expecting u to answer

I looked at it.

I sent it before I could overthink it and ruin the whole thing.

For a few awful seconds, nothing happened.

My screen showed Delivered.

No answer came.

I told myself that was fine.

That I deserved that.

That I had said I wasn't expecting one.

I checked my phone again three minutes later like a complete liar.

Still nothing.

Outside my window, the neighborhood looked normal. Porch lights. Dark rooftops. The glow from TVs through half-closed blinds. Three houses down, Ava's house sat quiet except for the upstairs bathroom light turning on and then off again.

Three houses.

That was all.

Not far enough to be strangers.

Way too close to pretend this didn't matter.

I set my phone on my nightstand and rolled onto my side.

I kept thinking about what my mom had said.

That embarrassment about being caught wasn't the same as being sorry for being cruel.

I wished I could stop thinking about that sentence.

I also knew I wouldn't since it was true.

And because the more I replayed everything, the clearer it became that the worst part wasn't the group chat.

Not really.

The worst part was that when I got mad, I had reached for the meanest version of Ava like it was already waiting in my head.

Which meant this was not just a texting problem.

It was a me problem.

And those are a lot harder to unsend.

A Full Apology

Mia Continued:

Two things were clear by Friday morning.

First: there is no such thing as casually checking a school group chat after you've publicly ruined your life in it.

Second: once you start thinking about sending another message to the same chat, your brain becomes a haunted house.

I checked PANTHER PRIDE 8TH GRADE COMMUNITY before I was even fully awake, which was a terrible way to begin the day.

There was nothing in it except a reminder about fundraiser money and one teacher asking people to stop changing their profile pictures to memes during school hours.

Normal stuff.

Which should have been comforting.

Instead, it made me more nervous.

Because all that normality was just sitting there on top of what I had done, like the chat had shrugged and moved on while the rest of my body absolutely had not.

My phone buzzed again.

A text from Becca.

u alive

I went still.

Typed:

physically yes

She answered immediately.

emotionally

I thought about that.

pending

That got a:

fair

Then:

u coming to school or faking you have COVID

I almost smiled.

coming

brave or terrible judgment

hard to say

That, unfortunately, was accurate.

Downstairs, my mom was making toast and acting normal in that way parents do when they have already had the serious talk and are now waiting to see whether the lesson sticks.

"You sleep at all?" she asked.

"Sort of."

She slid a plate toward me. "You look tired."

"Encouraging."

"I'm not trying to encourage you. I'm describing your face."

I sat down and picked up a piece of toast even though I wasn't hungry.

My mom leaned against the counter. "You seem tense."

"Good read."

She gave me a look. "Mia."

I sighed. "I keep thinking about sending something in the chat."

She was quiet.

"What kind of something?"

"A correction. A better apology. I don't know."

My mom crossed her arms loosely. "Do you want to do that because it's right, or because you're tired of feeling awful?"

"Both," I said honestly.

That seemed to surprise her.

"Alright," she said. "That's at least honest."

The toast went untouched in my hand.

"The problem," I said, "is that if I send something, everybody sees it again."

"Yes."

"And if I don't, then I'm just letting everything sit there."

"Yes."

"That's not helpful."

"It's not meant to be helpful. It's meant to be true."

I hated when adults did that.

Or rather, I hated when they did it and it worked.

My mom came over and sat across from me. "Mia, a public mistake sometimes needs a public response. That doesn't mean the response has to be perfect. It means it has to be real."

There was that word again.

Real.

As if reality had not already done enough damage.

"What if people think I'm only doing it because I got in trouble?"

My mom lifted one shoulder. "Some of them probably will."

That made me look up.

She nodded. "You don't control that part."

"I hate that."

"I know."

My gaze dropped again.

The problem was, she was right.

And worse, she and Mr. Harlow and Jayden and probably half the emotionally functional population were all right in the same direction.

I could not control what people thought.

I could control whether I stayed quiet because I was embarrassed.

By the time I got to school, that thought had lodged itself in my chest like a thumbtack.

Not enough to stop me.

Enough to make everything uncomfortable.

Becca met me by my locker with the expression of somebody approaching a wild animal she loved but did not fully trust not to bite.

"You look deeply unwell," she said.

"Thank you."

"You're welcome."

I spun my locker combination too fast the first time. Then too slow. Then just leaned my forehead against the metal for one second hoping maybe if I became part of the locker, the day could not legally start.

Becca lowered her voice. "What's wrong?"

"I'm thinking about putting something in the chat."

She went still.

"That is either very brave," she said, "or absolutely insane."

"Yes."

"Which one?"

"I have no idea."

She adjusted the strap of her backpack. "What would you even say?"

That was a good question.

I had a clue what I'd say.

At least mostly.

I had an idea but not the exact words. Those still changed every four seconds. But I knew what I owed.

The truth.

That the rumor wasn't true.

That I repeated it.

That I made things worse.

That Ava didn't deserve it.

Simple in theory.

Terrible in practice.

"I don't know yet," I said.

Becca was quiet. Then: "If you do it, people are going to talk about it again."

"I know."

"And screenshot it."

"I know."

"And maybe make fun of it."

"I know."

She winced. "Sorry. That felt obvious while I was saying it."

"No, it's fine. Today my role in life is hearing my fears read back to me by people who care."

"That sounds healthy."

"It feels super healthy."

We started walking toward first period.

Halfway down the hall, I saw Ava at the far end with Tessa and Lila.

Just seeing her made my stomach tighten.

Ava glanced up.

Saw me.

Looked away.

No glare. No dramatic pause. Nothing obvious.

Just that.

And that made the whole hallway feel thinner.

By lunch, I had typed seven different versions of a message and deleted all of them.

One in English.

Two in math.

One during a bathroom break that felt especially pathetic.

Three more while pretending to listen to Coach Mendez explain why half the class had somehow forgotten how to jog in a straight line.

Every version had some problem.

Too short.

Too defensive.

Too formal.

Too emotional.

Too much about me.

Not enough about Ava.

And underneath all of that was the real fear:

If I said the wrong thing publicly twice in the same week, I might actually have to transfer.

At lunch, Becca slid into the seat across from me and set down her tray.

"Status report."

"I'm trapped in a nightmare run by thumbs."

"That feels specific."

"It is specific."

I pushed my fries around. "Nothing sounds right."

Becca took out her phone. "Do you want help?"

"No."

"Do you want help but are too proud to admit it?"

I met her eyes.

She nodded. "Great. Hand it over."

I hesitated.

Against every instinct for self-preservation, I passed her my phone.

She read the draft I had sitting in my notes app.

Her eyebrows went up a little.

"What?"

"Nothing. It's not bad."

I narrowed my eyes. "That tone means something is bad."

"It's not bad bad. It's just…" She looked up. "You still sound like you're trying to survive it instead of own it."

That landed more directly than I wanted.

"Ouch," I said. "Rude."

"True, though."

Unfortunately, yes.

She handed the phone back. "Say the true thing first. Not the careful thing."

I met her eyes.

"Wow," I said slowly. "You had one useful thought this week."

"I'm growing."

That almost made me laugh.

Almost.

I looked back down at the screen.

She was right.

I had been writing around the real point, trying to make it soft enough that it wouldn't hurt me too much on the way out.

Which was not exactly how accountability worked.

I deleted everything again.

Typed:

what i said about ava and jayden wasnt true

I looked at it.

Kept going.

i heard a rumor and repeated it and i made things worse

Still not enough.

My fingers hovered.

Then:

ava didnt deserve that and neither did jayden

That made my heartbeat pick up.

It felt a tiny bit of relief already.

I added one last line:

im sorry

The four lines sat there, waiting.

Becca leaned over my shoulder.

"Oh," she said quietly.

"What?"

"That sounds like you."

I didn't know if that was good or bad.

Before I could ask, somebody two seats down said, way too loudly, "Yo, Mia's writing her memoir."

A couple of people laughed.

My entire body went hot.

I locked my phone instantly.

Becca turned and said, "Wow, Connor, that was deeply unnecessary."

Connor lifted both hands. "I'm joking."

"Then get better jokes," she snapped.

A few people at the table suddenly found their lunch fascinating.

My face burned as I focused on my tray.

Exactly.

The exact thing I was afraid of.

Attention.

Commentary.

The feeling of every private nerve sitting exposed right under cafeteria lighting.

Becca leaned closer. "Ignore him."

"I hate this," I muttered.

"I know."

"I seriously hate this."

"I know."

She was quiet.

She said, "But if you let Connor-from-band determine your character arc, I'm going to lose respect for you."

I met her eyes.

That was so insulting it almost helped.

Almost.

When lunch ended, I still hadn't sent it.

By seventh period, my notes page had become a graveyard of deleted versions again.

By final bell, I was angry.

Not at Ava.

Not at Jayden.

Not even really at Connor.

At myself.

Because every time I got close, I backed off.

And that felt a little too much like the same selfishness, just wearing nicer clothes.

Outside after school, people were clustering by the buses and bike rack and curb pickup like always. The sky had that flat gray color that made everything feel colder than it was.

I stood near the side of the building with my backpack hanging off one shoulder and my phone in my hand.

Becca was next to me.

"Alright," she said. "Either send it or don't. But you are starting to look like someone waiting to defuse a bomb in a movie."

"Funny because that's exactly how this feels."

She glanced at my screen. "Do you want me to do it?"

"No!"

"Wow. Violent response."

I took a breath.

Another.

Across the lot, I saw Ava with Tessa and Lila.

A little farther off, Jayden was with Ryder.

Normal arrangement. Normal school afternoon. Normal except for the way my pulse was climbing into my ears.

I looked down at my phone again.

Read the four lines one more time.

And before I could think better of it, I hit send.

For one second, nothing happened.

The message appeared in PANTHER PRIDE 8TH GRADE COMMUNITY under my name.

what i said about ava and jayden wasnt true

i heard a rumor and repeated it and i made things worse

ava didnt deserve that and neither did jayden im sorry

Every part of me went cold.

"Oh my gosh," Becca whispered.

"Yep."

"You did it."

"Yep."

There are moments where time slows down, and then there are moments where your body just panics so hard it fakes time slowing down for you.

This was the second kind.

My thumb twitched toward the screen like deleting it was still a thing that would solve any part of my life.

Too late.

Ryder's phone buzzed.

Tessa's.

Lila's.

Because the universe had a cruel sense of symmetry, Ava looked down at her phone.

Jayden.

Three different kids near the bus line.

The world did not stop.

It just bent toward the same point all at once.

I wanted to walk directly into traffic.

Nobody said anything for three full seconds.

That might not sound long, but in public-humiliation time it was a month.

The chat updated.

Ms. Ortega: Thank you for correcting the information. Let's all move forward respectfully.

That took a second to process.

Becca made a face. "That is such a teacher response."

"It's horrible."

"It's very on brand, though."

Another buzz.

Ryder: dang

Another:

Sophie: mk wow

Then:

Derek: respect honestly

I blinked once.

Becca blinked too. "Did Derek just become a person?"

"Nah it takes more than this."

Across the lot, Ava still had her phone in her hand.

She looked up.

Straight at me.

And since my life seemed determined to be as uncomfortable as possible, Jayden looked up at the exact same time.

For one second, all three of us were just standing there connected by terrible technology and the world's worst timing.

Lila said something to Ava.

Ava looked back down.

Tessa leaned closer to her.

Jayden glanced at Ryder, said something short, then looked at me one more time.

Like he was seeing what I had done and not making up his mind about it too quickly.

That should not have mattered.

It did.

My phone buzzed again.

A direct text from a number I didn't recognize.

bold move

I blinked hard while staring at it.

Immediately blocked the number because I had reached my daily limit for mystery opinions.

Becca's phone buzzed too. She checked it and grimaced. "Uh, bad news."

"What?"

"People are already sending screenshots of your apology. I think they've turned it into a meme."

I shut my eyes.

Naturally, they were.

The apology itself had become content.

The problem with public honesty, it turned out, was that it was still public.

"What are they saying?" I asked.

Becca hesitated.

I opened my eyes. "Becca."

She made a face. "Mixed stuff."

"That is not a real answer."

"Some people think it was good."

"And?"

"And some people think you only did it because you got in trouble."

The exact thing I had been afraid of.

And hearing it out loud didn't even hurt as much as I thought it would.

By now, the fear had been sitting in me so long it had already shaped itself to the space.

The chat was still open.

At my words.

At the fact that they were out there now, not fixable, not retractable, not private.

Even if people mocked it, the truth was still in the room now.

Ava did not deserve it.

Jayden did not deserve it.

I had made it worse.

That part could not be untold anymore.

"Okay," I said quietly.

Becca looked at me. "Okay?"

"Yeah."

"You don't seem as horrified as I expected."

"I'm still horrified."

"Then why do you sound weirdly calm?"

I thought about that.

Looked across the lot one more time.

Ava was talking to Tessa and Lila.

Jayden had gotten on his bike.

The buses were starting to load.

And under all the humiliation and panic and secondhand opinions flying around on phones, there was one small irritating fact:

I felt a tiny bit better.

"I think," I said slowly, "I'm just tired of letting the worst version of this be the loudest one."

Becca stared at me.

"That was extremely deep for somebody standing next to Bus 12."

"Don't ruin it."

"No promises."

We started walking toward the buses.

My phone buzzed again.

This time it was from Ava.

My whole body went alert.

I opened it.

Just two lines.

i saw it

thank you for saying it

I stopped walking.

Becca almost walked into me. "What?"

The screen glowed back at me.

No forgiveness.

No warmth exactly.

No instant emotional repair montage.

Just that.

I saw it.

Thank you for saying it.

And that felt bigger than a paragraph would have.

"What?" Becca asked again.

I looked up at her.

"Ava texted me."

Her eyes widened. "And?"

I held up the screen.

She read it and exhaled through her teeth. "k."

"k?"

"That's not nothing."

I looked back at the message.

No.

It wasn't.

Not even close.

I climbed onto the bus with my stomach still twisted and my face still warm and at least ten new things to overthink before dinner.

But finally all week, the panic had company.

Something smaller.

Not relief exactly.

Just the faint, unfamiliar sense that maybe doing the right thing badly was still better than doing nothing at all.

Origins

Mia Continued:

The problem with funny people is that they can make almost anything bearable for about six minutes.

After that, the actual problem is still there.

By Tuesday, Becca and I were speaking normally again, which should have felt good.

Instead, it felt like one of those movies where the background looks normal until you realize something in the wallpaper is blinking.

She was still Becca.

I was still me.

School was still school.

But now there was this extra layer underneath everything, like all our conversations had a hidden tab open.

I noticed it in dumb places.

The way she paused before bringing up Ava's name.

The way I wondered who else had already heard what before I accidentally sent it to the whole grade.

The way both of us had started checking our phones less casually, like they might bite.

By second period, I was already in a bad mood.

A boy in math had asked Connor if he'd found his hoodie yet, and Connor had said, "No, but at least I didn't announce it to the entire school."

Which was not technically about me.

I spent the rest of class pretending to take notes while mentally planning his downfall.

At lunch, I found Becca by our table opening a bag of chips like it had personally offended her.

"Hey," she said.

"Hey."

I sat down and immediately knew I was not going to make it through the meal acting normal.

Becca glanced up. "You look like you're either about to shed tears or commit arson."

"That might be a tad dramatic."

"It feels accurate."

I stabbed a fry with more force than necessary.

Becca watched me for two seconds, then sighed. "What?"

I met her eyes.

At my tray.

Back at her.

"You told Taylor."

Her face changed instantly.

Not guilty exactly.

But close enough to count.

"Mia—"

"No, I know it wasn't the exact message," I said quickly. "I know. But you still told her."

Becca set the chips down. "I told her part of it."

"Right."

"She was already asking."

I laughed once.

"That is literally how every bad decision at this school starts."

She looked down. "I know."

The problem was, I had already told myself I wasn't going to make this into some giant righteous speech. Because obviously the main explosion was still mine. Obviously, I had done the worst part.

But once I started thinking about it, I couldn't stop.

"She knew enough that by the time I freaked out and texted you, it wasn't even really just between us anymore," I said.

Becca nodded once. "Probably."

Probably.

That word made me want to throw a juice box.

"Becca."

"What do you want me to say?"

I met her eyes.

"I want you to say it was messed up," I said. "Not in a tiny oops way. In a real way."

She leaned back in her chair.

I thought she was going to get defensive.

Instead, she said, quietly, "It was messed up."

That took some of the air out of me immediately.

I still felt angry.

Just less justified.

"I shouldn't have repeated any of it," she said. "I know that."

"Then why did you?"

She gave a small, humorless laugh. "I guess because it's me?"

That should have been funny.

It wasn't.

"I don't know," she said. "Because it felt like one of those things everybody was already sort of saying. Taylor acts like she knows everything and I wanted to know if she'd heard more. I wasn't thinking about it like it was dangerous yet."

Right there.

Dangerous.

That was the right word.

That was what we had all missed at first.

That it was dangerous.

To Ava.

To Jayden.

To me.

To anybody dumb enough to trust the wrong audience with the wrong mood.

My gaze dropped to the table.

"I wasn't thinking about it like that either," I admitted.

Becca nodded. "I know."

We sat there in the kind of silence that isn't exactly comfortable but isn't pretending anymore either.

Around us, the cafeteria kept going. Trays clattering. Someone laughing too hard at the far table. A teacher asking three boys to stop standing on chairs since even social collapse had not made everyone smarter.

Finally, Becca said, "Do you want the honest version?"

"That depends on whether it's terrible."

"It is."

"Then yes."

She folded her arms on the table. "I think part of the reason I didn't stop it is because I knew you meant it."

That landed harder than I expected.

I lifted my gaze slowly.

"What does that mean?"

Becca held my gaze. "It means if you'd sent me some totally random rant about a person you didn't really care about, I probably would've rolled my eyes and told you to calm down. But you sounded… loaded."

Loaded.

Great.

Love that for me.

I met her eyes.

"You'd clearly been annoyed for a while," she said. "So, it didn't feel random. It felt like something you'd been waiting to say."

I turned away first.

That part I could not argue with.

Not really.

She was right.

The text had been fast.

But the irritation hadn't been.

That had been sitting there.

Collecting.

Stacking itself into little silent judgments every time Ava got too much attention, or too much sympathy, or ended up in the center of something again.

And yeah, if I was being honest, every time Jayden's name got attached to her, that only made it worse.

I picked at the corner of my napkin.

"It's not like I sat around plotting against her," I muttered.

"I know."

"Then why does it suddenly sound like I did?"

"Because," Becca said gently, "when stuff stays inside long enough, it doesn't really matter whether you planned it. It still builds."

That was so irritatingly true that I almost got up and left just to avoid having to hear the rest of it.

Instead, I stayed.

Unfortunately.

I looked across the cafeteria without really seeing anything.

Ava was at her usual table with Tessa and Lila.

She tipped her head back laughing at something Lila said, and I saw the old version of things.

Not even old-old.

Just a year ago.

Walking to school while it was warmer out.

Arguing about whether slushies counted as lunch.

Her sitting on my bedroom floor stealing my purple marker after hers had dried out.

Me going over to her house and knowing where the extra chips were before her mom even offered.

That part nobody else got.

How weird it was to be publicly not alright with someone you used to be privately ordinary with.

I must've been staring too long, because Becca said, "You miss her."

I turned to her sharply. "That is not what's happening."

Becca gave me a look that would have been insulting if it weren't so boringly accurate.

"Okay," she said.

I hated that okay.

"You make it sound like I want everything to go back to normal," I said.

"Don't you?"

I opened my mouth.

Wisely shut it again.

I didn't want to go backward.

Backward meant pretending the resentment hadn't been there.

Pretending I hadn't been unfair.

Pretending she hadn't been hurt.

Pretending neighborhood history automatically meant friendship.

That part was over.

But I also didn't want this.

Whatever this was.

The stiffness.

The caution.

The weird little moments in the hallway where one of us said a sentence and the other one had to decide whether it was safe to answer like a person.

"I don't know what I want," I said finally.

Becca nodded slowly. "That's probably more honest."

I rested my elbows on the table and pressed my hands against my forehead.

"This is exhausting."

Becca let out a breath through her nose. "Please don't ever use that word again."

I lifted my gaze.

She grimaced. "Sorry. Bad joke."

I held her gaze for one second longer.

Against my will, I laughed.

Which, unfortunately, was very Becca.

She pointed at me. "See? We're healing."

"We are absolutely not healing."

"Somewhat functioning, then."

"Barely."

That was when someone slid into the empty seat at the far end of our table.

Connor-from-band.

Naturally.

He opened his milk and said, "So are we all cool again or is this still, like, a thing?"

Becca and I turned to him at the exact same time.

I could actually feel something in my face go blank.

"Connor," Becca said, in a voice so flat it almost echoed, "I need you to develop fear."

He blinked.

I said, "Also shame."

He looked between us. "What? I was just asking."

"About something that is none of your business," I said.

He held up one hand. "Now."

"No," Becca said. "Not wow. Just stop using people's lives like lunch entertainment."

Connor muttered something about everyone being sensitive and got up to leave.

I watched him go.

Looked back at Becca.

We both sat there for one second in complete silence.

And then we started laughing.

Becca wiped under one eye. "I hate him."

"I know."

"He walked into that like he was hosting a panel."

"I know."

That laugh faded fast, but it left the air a little less tight.

Becca leaned her chin into her hand. "Can I say one more annoying true thing?"

"No."

"I'm going to anyway."

"Of course you are."

She looked at Ava's table, then back at me. "I don't think your real problem is whether Ava forgives you."

I frowned. "Then what is it?"

"I think your real problem is that she might forgive you and still not want the same kind of friendship back."

That one was like a punch to the gonads.

Harder than anything else she'd said all lunch.

Buried under all my guilt and embarrassment and overthinking, I think I had still been picturing some version of the future where if I said the right things, meant them enough, and survived enough humiliation, eventually everything would settle.

Not exactly back to normal.

But close enough to recognize.

I saw what Becca meant.

That even if Ava believed me…

even if she stopped being mad…

even if the rumor finally died…

that still wouldn't mean we went back.

This had revealed too much.

My hands went still in my lap.

"That sucks," I said quietly.

Becca nodded. "Yeah."

After lunch, I walked to English alone. My emotional support comedian had already done her shift for the day.

The hallway was crowded and loud and smelled like gym shoes and somebody's way-too-strong vanilla body spray.

I saw Ava at the water fountain ahead of me.

Just her.

No Tessa. No Lila. No convenient buffer.

She looked up as I got closer.

For one second, I considered pretending I needed something from my locker and fleeing sideways into another hallway like a cowardly crab.

Instead, I kept walking.

Owing to the fact that public mistakes do not magically make you better at normal human interaction. They just remove your excuses.

"Ava," I said.

She straightened a little.

Not defensive exactly.

Just alert.

"Hey," she said.

That word again.

Hey.

The most useless possible syllable and still everybody's favorite.

I stopped a few feet away.

Not close-close.

Just enough to count as an actual conversation if one happened.

"I wasn't trying to ignore you at lunch," I said.

Ava blinked once. "Fine."

"I know that sounds random."

"It does."

I exhaled. "I just meant—things are weird."

One corner of her mouth moved, not quite into a smile.

"That is the most accurate thing you've said to me all week."

Honestly, fair.

I looked down the hall for one second, then back at her.

"I'm trying not to make it worse."

Ava was quiet.

She said, "I know."

That helped.

A little.

Enough to keep going.

"I don't expect you to just be over it."

"Good," she said, not meanly.

"Yeah." I gave one small nod. "I figured."

The bell hadn't rung yet, but people were starting to move around us in quicker currents now, that pre-class shuffle where everyone suddenly remembered time existed.

Ava shifted her backpack strap higher on her shoulder.

"I believe you feel bad," she said.

I lifted my gaze.

She held my gaze. "That's not the same thing as me knowing what to do with it yet."

The whole chapter in one sentence.

Not whether she believed me.

What came after belief.

I gave a slow nod. "Fine."

Ava glanced toward her classroom door. "Fine."

She walked off.

No dramatic ending.

No repair montage.

No giant speech.

Just two fines in a hallway that still felt too bright.

I stood there until somebody bumped my shoulder and muttered, "Sorry."

I went to English.

That night, I sat on my bed with homework open and my phone face-down beside me and tried to imagine what life would feel like if I stopped thinking about every single social interaction like it might secretly be a test.

Probably peaceful.

Probably unavailable to me.

Outside, the neighborhood looked exactly the same as it always had. Porch lights. Dark trees. A basketball hoop in somebody's driveway. The sidewalk Ava and I had walked down a hundred times over the years, now somehow carrying way more history than concrete should be allowed to.

My phone buzzed once.

A text from Becca.

for the record i have developed fear and shame

I went still.

Laughed.

Typed back:

growth looks good on u

She answered immediately:

dont get used to it

I set the phone down again and leaned back against the wall.

Becca had been right about something else too.

This did not start with one message.

The message just yanked everything private into public light.

And now the hard part wasn't saying sorry.

It was facing what the sorry had uncovered.

That I'd let old irritation harden into cruelty.

That I had wanted someone to agree with the worst version of Ava.

That neighborhood history did not excuse any of that.

And maybe hardest of all—

That wanting things fixed didn't mean I got to choose what fixed looked like.

Reality

Ava:

I had become deeply suspicious of any adult who used the phrase good opportunity.

Especially if they said it with a calm face.

Ms. Howard had said it that morning when she announced our English presentation groups.

"Since this is a good opportunity," she said, smiling in the way teachers do when they are about to ruin your week in the name of character-building, "I've made the groups for you."

That should have been my warning.

Instead, I had been busy putting my name on the top of my paper and trying not to think about the fact that there were now two separate social storylines about me floating around the grade. One was still the old rumor. The other was whether Mia and I were in some kind of dramatic reconciliation process, which was news to me.

Ms. Howard started reading the groups.

"Tessa, Ryan, and Maya."

Fine.

"Lila, Connor, and Becca."

Honestly, hilarious for all the wrong reasons.

Then:

"Ava, Mia, and Nolan."

I actually looked up so fast I almost gave myself whiplash.

Across the room, Mia had the exact same expression.

Nolan, who sat two rows over and had become a giant human golden retriever in jeans, looked delighted just to be included in anything.

"Cool," he whispered to no one.

I stared at Ms. Howard.

She smiled at the room like she had just solved world peace using color-coded index cards.

I wanted to raise my hand and say, respectfully, this is not a good opportunity. This is a social experiment with minors.

I did not.

I enjoy dignity in theory.

Still, for the rest of class, my notes on persuasive speaking looked like they had been written by someone riding a bus over potholes.

As soon as the bell rang, Tessa turned in her seat so fast I thought she might launch herself into the aisle.

"No way," she whispered.

"That is exactly what I was thinking," I whispered back.

Lila came up beside my desk. "Maybe it'll be good?"

I met her eyes.

She made a face. "Wow. Never mind."

Across the room, Becca had both hands over her mouth and looked like she was trying not to react in a way that would get her personally kicked out of school.

Mia was putting her notebook into her backpack very carefully, which looked more stressed than if she'd thrown it at the wall.

Nolan walked over to us with the blissful confidence of somebody who had absolutely no idea he had just been placed in the middle of an emotional minefield.

"So," he said brightly, "should we split up the work or meet after school?"

Tessa physically turned away and coughed into her sleeve.

Lila looked at the ceiling.

I closed my eyes for one second.

Mia said, "We can split it up."

At the same exact time, I said, "Maybe we should meet."

We both stopped.

Nolan blinked between us.

"Right," he said slowly. "That feels like something we should maybe decide together."

I turned to Mia.

She looked back.

Neither of us seemed excited to be doing this in front of an audience.

"Library after school?" Mia said.

There was a tiny pause before the question mark part, like even she wasn't fully sure she had the right to suggest anything.

That annoyed me less than it should have.

"Fine," I said.

"Cool," Nolan said, way too cheerfully. "Awesome. Great. We're already collaborating."

Tessa made a sound that was either a laugh or a near-death experience.

The rest of the day, I tried not to think about the fact that I was going to have to sit at a table with Mia and discuss presentation slides like we were just two normal classmates with no shared history and no recent emotional crater.

That worked exactly zero percent.

By the time last period ended, I had managed to become irritated at Ms. Howard, Mia, group projects, school, the educational system, and the basic concept of persuasive speaking.

The library always smelled like dust, printer paper, and old carpet.

Which felt like exactly the right place for forced emotional maturity.

Nolan got there first and had already claimed a table near the back by the nonfiction section. He had his Chromebook open and two pens lined up in front of him like he was preparing for surgery.

Mia arrived right after me.

For one horrible second, we both reached for the same chair.

Both stopped.

Both stepped back.

Nolan looked up and said, "I can sit over here."

Neither of us answered.

He moved anyway.

I sat down across from Mia.

There should honestly be a law requiring one deeply neutral person for situations like this, and Nolan was doing a public service without even knowing it.

"So," he said, clapping his hands once quietly. "The topic is whether students should have more choice in elective classes."

"I'm already persuaded," I muttered.

To my surprise, Mia almost smiled.

It was brief.

Still.

Nolan nodded like this was all going very well. "Perfect. We need an intro, main points, examples, and a closing."

He started assigning things with the confidence of a substitute teacher who doesn't yet know the class is impossible.

"I can do the opening," he said. "Mia, maybe examples? Ava, maybe the main points?"

"Sure," I said.

"Fine," Mia said.

Again.

Sure.

Fine.

Alright.

The whole emotional vocabulary of people trying not to explode in public.

For twenty minutes, we actually worked.

Not well or even smoothly.

But enough.

Nolan typed. I pulled up district elective info on my Chromebook. Mia found examples from the student survey Ms. Howard had made us fill out last month. If you blurred the edges hard enough, we might even have looked like a normal group.

Nolan got called away by the librarian because he had checked out a book two weeks ago and was now on some kind of literary watchlist.

"I'll be right back," he said, hurrying off.

And just like that, my human buffer was gone.

The silence hit immediately.

Mia looked at her screen.

I checked mine.

Neither of us typed anything for a full ten seconds.

Mia said, "You can switch with me if you want."

I lifted my gaze. "What?"

"The project part." She pointed at my screen. "The main points. If you don't want to do that."

"Oh."

It took me a second to understand that she was just trying to make something easier.

"I'm fine," I said.

She nodded. "Right."

There was that word again.

I don't know why it kept getting to me so much.

Maybe because right was what people said when they wanted to sound calm enough not to scare the room.

I looked back down at my screen.

Before I could talk myself out of it, I said, "This is weird."

Mia let out a short breath through her nose. "Yeah."

That should have been the end of it.

Instead, I kept going.

"Like… not just because of everything."

She was quiet.

Then: "I know."

I lifted my gaze again.

Mia's eyes were on the table now, not on me.

She tapped her finger once against the edge of her Chromebook.

"It was weird before," she said.

The sentence landed.

The sentence sitting underneath half this book.

I leaned back in my chair.

"How long?" I asked.

Mia looked up.

"How long what?"

"How long has it been weird?"

That was not a fair question.

Which was probably why I asked it.

She looked genuinely unsure.

She said, carefully, "I don't know. A while."

That answer annoyed me immediately.

"A while," I repeated.

"I said I don't know."

"That's not an answer."

She straightened a little. "Then what do you want? A date?"

I folded my arms.

"No," I said. "I want to know whether I'm supposed to be surprised."

The second it came out, I knew it was meaner than I meant it to be.

Mia flinched anyway.

"I'm not asking just to make you feel worse," I said.

She gave me a look. "That's convenient."

"Wow."

"Sorry." She looked down again. "No. Not sorry exactly. Just—I don't know. This is not easy."

"I know."

She laughed once, quietly, and there was no humor in it. "Yeah. That feels like the theme."

Neither of us said anything.

The librarian rolled a cart by in the next aisle.

Someone's printer job started up at the front desk.

Nolan was still gone, probably being questioned about overdue books like he was running some kind of underground novel ring.

Mia rubbed her thumb against the edge of her pencil.

"I think," she said slowly, "it got weird when everything stopped being simple and we kept pretending it wasn't."

I frowned.

She kept going, still not looking at me.

"When we were little, we just… lived next to each other. That was enough. Then we got older and had different people and different stuff and it stopped feeling automatic. But we still acted like it was."

That landed harder than I wanted it to.

That was exactly part of it.

I looked down at my screen.

"I didn't know you were mad," I said.

Mia was quiet. "I don't think I knew I was either. Not really."

That sounded like a lie at first.

It sounded like the truth.

Which was more annoying.

"I was annoyed sometimes," she said. "And jealous sometimes. And unfair in my head a lot more than I should've been."

My throat tightened.

The library suddenly felt too warm.

"At least that's honest," I muttered.

She nodded once. "Yeah."

I should have hated hearing that.

Instead, I mostly hated how much I'd already guessed it.

The text had hurt, but it also hadn't felt random. Not fully. It had felt like somebody finally saying the ugly version out loud.

"What about you?" Mia asked.

I lifted my gaze.

"What?"

She hesitated. "Were you… mad too? Before all this?"

There are some questions that are rude mostly because they are late.

That was one of them.

I leaned back farther in my chair and looked at the ceiling.

"Yes," I said.

Mia blinked. "At me?"

"Yes."

She actually looked startled.

That helped in a petty way I am not proud of.

"You always acted like it didn't matter if plans changed," I said. "Or if I ended up left out of something. Or if you got quiet for like a week and then came back acting normal again."

Her expression shifted.

I could tell she was replaying things now.

Good.

"You make it sound like I was doing that on purpose," she said.

"I don't know if you were."

"That's not an answer either."

I almost smiled at that, but I respected myself enough not to.

"I think," I said slowly, "we both got used to just assuming the other person would still be there."

Mia looked at me for a long second.

Nodded.

"I guess."

I hated how much that felt like progress.

Nolan came back then, carrying a library pass and looking deeply confused about why the air at our table had changed shape while he was gone.

"Did I miss something?" he asked, sitting down.

"No," Mia and I said at the same time.

Nolan looked between us.

Wisely, said, "Cool."

For the rest of the meeting, we worked better.

But now there was less pretending in the room.

By the time we packed up, our outline was finished and Nolan seemed genuinely pleased with us, which felt like being congratulated for surviving minor surgery.

As we left the library, he headed toward the buses and waved over his shoulder.

"See you guys tomorrow."

Mia and I walked the same direction. We did. Naturally. We were neighbors.

Outside, the air had turned colder. The sky was starting to dim into that flat evening gray where the whole street looked softer than it really was.

For the first half block, neither of us spoke.

Mia said, "I'm glad you told me."

I glanced at her. "About what?"

"That you were mad too."

I shoved my hands into my hoodie pocket. "You looked way too surprised."

She looked down. "I know."

"That was annoying."

"I know."

Again.

I know.

This time, it didn't sound defensive.

It just sounded tired.

We reached the corner where our paths technically split for all of twenty feet before becoming the same sidewalk again.

Mia stopped.

"I'm not asking you to just get over it," she said.

I met her eyes.

"I know."

"No, I mean it." She shifted her backpack higher. "I know I keep saying sorry, and I mean it every time, but I know that doesn't just automatically fix…" She gestured vaguely between us. "Any of this."

I gave a slow nod.

That helped more than I wanted it to.

What I was most tired of, maybe, was everybody acting like apologies were tiny magical keys that unlocked instant closure if you just used enough of them.

"I'm not trying to drag it out," I said.

"I know."

I exhaled.

Three houses away.

That was the dumbest part.

You can't dramatically storm out of a life that close.

Your moms still wave from driveways even when you wish they wouldn't.

Mia looked toward my house, then back at me.

"So… project tomorrow?"

That was such a normal question it almost made me laugh.

"Yeah," I said.

We stood there one second too long.

She headed toward her driveway and I headed toward mine.

Halfway up the walk, I looked back.

She had already gone inside.

I unlocked my front door and stepped into the smell of garlic and onions from dinner starting on the stove.

My mom called, "How was the library?"

I set my backpack down.

"Educational," I said.

She leaned around the corner. "In a good way?"

I thought about the project.

The conversation.

The fact that none of this was fixed and also none of it felt exactly the same as yesterday.

I said, "In a weird way."

My mom nodded like that tracked. “And?”

I took off my shoes.

“And maybe it was a little useful.”

That got a small smile out of her.

I headed upstairs before she could ask anything more specific.

In my room, I dropped onto the bed and stared at the ceiling.

Mia and I were not better.

Not really.

But finally since the whole thing blew up, it felt like we were at least talking about the real problem.

The automatic version of friendship both of us had kept pretending still worked.

It would have been easier if the text had been a total accident with no history under it.

Instead, it had history all over it.

Which was terrible.

But maybe also the only reason any of this honesty was happening now.

I wasn’t ready to call that good.

Still.

It was something.

The New Version

Mia:

There should be a scientific term for the feeling of realizing a social disaster has developed a second head.

That was what Thursday felt like.

Not a new disaster exactly.

Just the old one finding a fresh way to embarrass me.

The first clue came before first period, when I was at my locker and two girls from homeroom passed by talking in that fake-casual voice people use when they absolutely want to be overheard.

"I mean, it makes more sense now."

"Right? Like why else would she even care that much?"

They didn't look at me.

I stared into my locker for a full five seconds after they walked away, even though there was nothing in there I actually needed.

Behind me, Becca said, "Hey, I saw that."

I shut the locker. "Cool."

"That was terrible."

"I know."

She adjusted the strap on her bag. "Do you want me to trip them?"

"That would briefly improve my mood."

"See? I'm useful."

We started walking toward first period, but my whole body already had that hot, miserable buzz that meant the day had managed to become awful before 8:15.

The problem was, I knew this was coming.

I knew.

The second I apologized publicly, the story had to rearrange itself, and the easiest new version was obvious:

Mia likes Jayden.

That's why she cared.

That's why she hated Ava.

That's why the text happened.

That's why the apology happened.

Clean.

Simple.

Wrong in the way most school stories are wrong — by being just true enough in one corner to flatten everything else.

Which was almost more embarrassing than if it were made up.

Okay yes, I liked Jayden.

Now.

Apparently.

Or maybe before. I still wasn't thrilled about the timeline.

But that wasn't the whole reason. It wasn't even the biggest one.

And I had absolutely no way to explain that to people without sounding like someone giving a TED Talk in her own defense.

By second period, I'd already caught Connor-from-band smirking at me twice and Ryder saying something to Mateo that ended with all three of them looking away too quickly when I passed.

That should have made me mad at them.

Instead, it mostly made me want to crawl under a desk and stay there until high school.

In English, Ms. Howard had us sit with our presentation groups again, which meant I spent forty minutes next to Ava and Nolan trying to discuss elective classes while my brain kept replaying the phrase why else would she even care that much like it had rented space in my skull.

Nolan was talking about adding statistics to our opening slide.

Ava was making bullet points on her Chromebook.

I was staring at the same sentence in my notes for so long it had stopped looking like language.

"Mia?"

I blinked once.

Ava was looking at me.

"What?"

Nolan frowned a little. "Everything good?"

That question should be illegal at school.

"No," I said before I could stop myself.

Both of them went quiet.

I realized what I'd just said.

"I mean—yeah. Sorry. I'm fine."

Ava gave me a look that made it clear she did not believe me for one second.

Neither did Nolan, but he was polite enough to pretend.

I looked back at my screen and tried to focus.

It almost worked.

Ten minutes later, a folded note landed on the table between me and Ava.

Just like that.

Like we were in a bad movie about children.

Nolan reached for it first, confused.

Ava got there faster.

She unfolded it.

I watched her eyes move once across the page.

Her whole expression flattened.

"What?" Nolan asked.

Ava looked at me.

She handed me the note.

In slanted pencil, it said: *ask jayden if he wants to help w ur project too lol*

For one second, the note seemed to fill the whole room.

Another.

The room around me went weirdly far away.

"Oh my gosh," Nolan said quietly.

Ava folded the note back up once and set it on the table like it was something gross she didn't want to touch too long.

I looked toward the back of the room.

Three boys by the windows suddenly found their notebooks incredibly interesting.

Ms. Howard was helping someone near the front and hadn't seen any of it.

Naturally, she hadn't.

There are some humiliations school will always make sure happen unsupervised.

Nolan said, "Do you want me to say something?"

I almost laughed.

"No," I said.

The word came out flat.

Ava's eyes were still on me.

"You don't have to pretend that's not awful," she said quietly.

That got me.

Obviously.

That was my whole thing lately.

Pretending things were manageable until they became medically concerning.

I looked down at the note again.

"No," I said. "It's awful."

Nolan sat back. "People are so weird."

That was true, but not enough to help.

What actually made it hurt wasn't just the note itself.

It was that this was the version now.

Not Mia sent a bad text.

Not Mia hurt Ava.

Not Mia was wrong.

Now it was Mia likes Jayden, therefore nothing she did counts as morally complicated anymore. To everyone else, girls with crushes were automatically ridiculous, and everybody seemed to find that very relaxing.

The bell rang before I had to say anything else.

I stuffed the note into my binder instead of throwing it away.

As we left the room, Nolan said, "Seriously, I can tell Ms. Howard if you want."

"Don't."

"Mia—"

"Please just don't."

He glanced at Ava.

Ava looked at me.

I shook my head once.

Nolan nodded. "Okay."

He peeled off toward history.

That left me and Ava walking out into the hallway together.

For one second, I considered speeding up or slowing down, anything to avoid being next to her while my face still felt like a fever.

But she was going the same direction.

So, sidewalk rules.

We were both stuck with it.

"I'm sorry," Ava said after a few steps.

I met her eyes.

That was not what I expected.

"You're sorry?"

"For the note. Not because I wrote it, obviously."

That almost got a laugh out of me, which would have been a very strange emotional choice.

I looked ahead. "Thanks."

Ava shoved a loose strand of hair behind her ear. "People are idiots."

I breathed out through my nose. "That has become the main theme of my life."

"Fair."

We kept walking.

Ava said, "It's not really fair."

I glanced over. "What?"

She looked straight ahead when she answered.

"That they're acting like that explains everything."

That stopped me internally.

My throat tightened. "Yeah."

"It's not like…" She hesitated, clearly irritated at herself for even having to say this. "It's not like you only said that stuff because of Jayden."

My face went hot again.

I didn't know whether to be grateful or horrified that Ava, of all people, was the one defending the complexity of my bad decisions.

"No," I said quietly. "I didn't."

Ava nodded once.

After a second: "You were unfair. But it wasn't random."

The truest, worst summary.

Unfair.

Not random.

My gaze dropped to the floor tiles as we walked.

"Yeah."

Ava slowed at her classroom door. "For what it's worth, I don't think the crush part makes it less serious."

I lifted my gaze.

She gave one tiny shrug. "If anything, people are using it to make it dumber than it actually was."

She went inside.

I stood there in the hallway after she disappeared, feeling like someone had just handed me my own insides in a labeled box.

At lunch, I made the mistake of sitting down.

That sounds dramatic, but what I mean is this: the second I sat, Sophie slid into the seat next to Becca and said, way too brightly, "So are we acknowledging the Jayden thing now or no?"

I met her eyes.

Becca looked at her.

The whole table sort of paused in that awful social way where no one wants to be first to say this is insane, because then suddenly, they're part of the moment.

Sophie lifted both hands. "I'm just saying, everybody already knows."

Becca turned slowly. "Do you hear yourself when you talk?"

Sophie blinked. "Wow."

"No," Becca said. "Not wow. Stop acting like Mia is a topic."

That should have solved it.

Instead, Sophie leaned back and gave me the exact expression people use when they think they are being understanding while actually making everything ten times worse.

"I'm not judging you," she said. "I'm just saying it makes sense."

There are very few phrases in the English language more dangerous than it makes sense.

What it really means is: I have decided on your motives and would now like credit for being compassionate about them.

I put my tray down.

Had not even taken a bite.

Already spiritually exhausted.

"It doesn't make sense," I said.

Sophie frowned. "What?"

"This." I gestured vaguely, because if I got more specific, I was going to start setting furniture on fire. "You all keep acting like one thing explains everything."

She blinked. "I didn't say everything."

"You implied it."

Becca murmured, "And scene."

I ignored her.

Sophie crossed her arms. "Okay, then explain it."

That was what I hated.

The fake invitation.

As if I owed the room a better script for my own humiliation.

I looked around the table.

Half of them were pretending not to listen. The other half had already committed.

"No," I said.

Sophie opened her mouth again.

Shut it.

Maybe even she realized there was no version of this where I gave a neat explanatory speech over school pizza and she came out looking normal.

She got up a minute later with a muttered, "Whatever."

The second she left, I stood too.

Becca looked up. "Where are you going?"

"Outside. Into the woods. Into witness protection."

"Mia."

I grabbed my tray. "I can't do this."

She stood up. "Do you want me to come?"

"No."

That came out too fast.

I took a breath. "No. I just need like… five minutes where nobody is trying to solve me."

Becca nodded.

That was one good thing about her. Under all the chaos, she usually knew when to stop chasing.

I dumped my tray and headed for the side doors near the gym, where there was a bench that technically wasn't for lunch but also wasn't not for lunch if no teacher cared enough to move you.

The sky outside had gone pale and thin; the kind of gray that made everything look colder than it was.

I sat down and pulled the folded note out of my binder.

Stared at it.

Folded it smaller.

Smaller again.

Still didn't throw it away.

I couldn't. Part of me needed physical proof that this week had become a joke people could write down and pass around like candy.

I heard the door open behind me.

"Please tell me you're not here to say it makes sense."

I didn't turn around, but I knew who it was.

Jayden stopped a few feet away. "That was specific."

I lifted my gaze.

He had his lunch in one hand and that unreadable expression he had gotten lately whenever I was around, like he was trying to be fair on purpose.

"I'm having a rough day," I said.

"Yeah. I noticed."

He sat down at the far end of the bench without asking, which should have annoyed me but didn't.

We just sat there in the cold, both looking out at the side parking lot like maybe a life-changing answer would emerge from the line of teacher cars.

He glanced at the paper in my hand.

"What's that?"

I thought about lying.

Handed it to him.

He read it.

His face changed immediately.

Not in a huge way.

But still.

"That's dumb," he said.

I gave a short laugh. "You keep saying that like it's new information."

"It's still true."

He folded the note back up and handed it to me.

I thought that was all he was going to say.

Then: "People are being lazy."

I frowned. "What?"

"With you."

I met his eyes.

He leaned his elbows on his knees. "The whole 'oh she likes him so that explains everything' thing. It's lazy."

I don't know why that hit so hard.

Perhaps I had been thinking the same thing all day and hearing somebody else say it made it real.

Maybe since it was him.

"Thanks," I said quietly.

He shrugged once. "I mean, it's still a mess."

"Wow. Also, helpful."

"But I'm right."

I turned away. "Yeah."

A couple of eighth graders came out the side doors laughing too loudly about something unrelated and immediately got quieter when they saw us sitting there.

Naturally, they did.

Because why not.

Their eyes flicked from me to Jayden and back again before they kept walking.

I actually felt my whole body tense.

Jayden noticed.

His face went flat in that same way it had with Derek in the parking lot.

That was when I realized he was mad too.

Not just uncomfortable. Mad.

"See?" I muttered. "It's like I can't even exist near you without people making it weird."

Jayden was quiet.

He said, "Then stop letting them set the tone."

I met his eyes. "That sounds great in theory."

"It works in practice too."

"You say that like it's simple."

"It's not simple." He glanced toward the doors the other kids had gone through. "It's just better than letting the dumbest people in school write the story for everybody else."

Again.

Story.

Version.

Explanation.

Everybody had one.

Everybody wanted one.

And none of them were really about the truth. They were about convenience.

I rubbed my thumb against the folded note. "I'm tired."

"I know."

That word again.

I almost laughed.

"I'm serious," he said. "This week has been weird for me too. But it's been way worse for you and Ava."

I met his eyes.

It told me he understood the shape of things better than a lot of other people did.

"I don't know how to stop it," I said.

Jayden looked out at the parking lot again. "You probably can't stop all of it."

"That's encouraging."

"But you can stop acting like every new version deserves to become your whole life."

I let that sit there.

It sounded almost annoyingly healthy.

"I hate how reasonable people are getting around me," I muttered.

That got a quick smile out of him.

He stood up.

"I gotta go," he said. "Coach already thinks I'm allergic to punctuality."

He started walking back toward the doors, then looked back once.

"And for the record," he said, "I never thought your apology was fake."

I met his eyes.

He shrugged. "Just seemed worth saying."

He went inside.

I sat there for another minute with the folded note in my hand and the cold pressing through the bench and the whole day still sitting on my shoulders like wet laundry.

What Ava had said in the hall.

What Jayden had just said.

What Becca had been saying for days in different forms.

Nobody I actually cared about was flattening this the way everyone else was.

That should have made me feel better.

Instead, it mostly made me realize how much energy I'd been spending fighting people who were never going to understand it right anyway.

By the time I went back inside, the lunch period was almost over.

Becca looked up the second she saw me.

"Everything good?"

"No."

I sat down and took my notebook out for next period.

Becca studied my face. "Did you cry?"

"What? No."

"You look like you almost had a thought."

I met her eyes.

She grinned a little. "Sorry. That was rude."

"It was also impressively annoying."

She leaned closer. "What happened?"

The folded note sat in my hands one more time.

At her.

Slid it across the table.

She unfolded it, read it, and made a face so immediate and disgusted it almost healed something in me.

"Oh, absolutely not."

"Yeah."

She looked up. "Who wrote this?"

"I don't know."

Becca crumpled it in her fist. "Cowards. If you're going to be terrible, at least develop handwriting courage."

That got me.

A tiny laugh. Still a laugh.

The bell rang right then, saving both of us from becoming too emotionally functional in public.

As we stood up, Becca bumped my shoulder lightly.

"For what it's worth," she said, "people doing this does not magically make all your actual feelings fake."

I met her eyes.

She shrugged. "I'm trying to be wise now. It's my thing, apparently."

That was such a ridiculous sentence I almost smiled again.

Almost.

By the time I got home, I was past angry and into that blank tired place where emotions stop lining up properly.

My mom asked how school was.

I said, "Annoying."

She said, "Specific."

And I went upstairs before the conversation could become educational.

That night, I lay on my bed staring at the ceiling with the note finally in the trash and my phone face-down beside me.

I kept thinking about what Ava had said.

You were unfair. But it wasn't random.

That was the sentence of the week, probably.

Maybe the sentence of the whole book if I was being dramatic.

Yes, the crush part was real enough to be embarrassing. And yes, people were using it to make me feel ridiculous. But the worst thing about all of this still wasn't that I liked Jayden.

It was that I had already been carrying around enough irritation and resentment that one rumor turned all of it into something cruel.

Liking him was not the whole story.

It wasn't even the best excuse.

And maybe that was why this new version bothered me so much.

It made everything smaller.

Dumber.

Easier to dismiss.

And I didn't want what I'd done dismissed.

I wanted it understood.

Even if understanding it made me look worse in other ways.

I rolled onto my side and looked out the window toward the dark line of houses down the street.

Ava's porch light was on.

Three houses away.

Same as always.

But now I could feel something changing.

Like the worst of it had not passed yet, but it was finally gathering shape.

And if the story was going to keep moving, then eventually I was going to have to do more than keep correcting people after they'd already said something dumb.

Eventually I was going to have to stop it while it was happening.

That thought sat with me long after the room went dark.

A Decision

Jayden:

I had developed a strong dislike for the phrase I'm just saying.

Mostly because nobody who said it was ever just saying anything.

They were suggesting.

Poking.

Trying out a version.

Lighting a match and pretending they were only there for warmth.

That morning, Ryder said it before first period while we were standing by the lockers.

"I'm just saying," he said, opening his backpack, "if people are still talking about it this much, then obviously nobody actually thinks it's over."

I met his eyes.

Mateo leaned against the locker next to mine. "That is not insightful. That's literally just the situation."

Ryder nodded. "Exactly. I'm the voice of the people."

"You are the voice of people who need hobbies," I said.

He grinned. "Still counts."

Normally that would've been the end of it.

A dumb hallway exchange.

Three guys talking before class.

Nothing worth remembering.

Except then Connor-from-band walked by and said, "Yo, ask Jayden if he wants to help with the presentation," and kept walking before I could answer.

Mateo muttered, "Wow."

Ryder looked after Connor. "Yeah, that one was bad."

I stared down the hallway.

It should not have gotten under my skin as much as it did.

I was tired of how easy people found it to turn other people's lives into loose material.

It wasn't just Mia anymore.

Or Ava.

Or even me.

It was the whole school's favorite little project now, and every person who added a joke or a comment or a fake-sympathetic I'm just saying got to act like they hadn't really contributed.

That part that bothered me most.

The pretending.

"I'm serious, though," Ryder said. "I don't think people even mean half of it."

I met his eyes. "That doesn't help."

"No, I know." He shifted his backpack higher. "I just mean they're bored."

Mateo shrugged. "Bored and cowards."

That was actually closer.

Boredom alone didn't make people say things louder when the actual person walked by.

It took something else too.

Distance, maybe.

Or the illusion of it.

The idea that if something was already public, then nobody adding one more comment really mattered.

We started walking toward class, and I spotted Mia at her locker farther down the hall.

She looked normal from a distance.

That was another thing school was good at.

Making people look fine from ten feet away.

As we got closer, I saw Connor say something to the guy next to him and glance in her direction. Not even subtle about it.

Mia shut her locker.

Almost slammed it shut.

Started walking the other way with Becca.

Ryder followed my eyes and said, quieter this time, "Yeah. That's getting old."

I met his eyes.

He lifted one shoulder. "What? I'm not a monster."

That was the thing with Ryder.

He actually wasn't.

He just liked living right up against the border between funny and annoying and then acting surprised when other people noticed the difference first.

In English, Ms. Howard made us keep working in our presentation groups, which meant I had front-row seats to Mia, Ava, and Nolan pretending to be a normal three-person academic unit.

From across the room, it almost worked.

Nolan was doing most of the talking because Nolan could talk to a brick wall and make it feel included.

Ava was typing.

Mia was reading from her laptop with the expression of someone trying not to emotionally combust in public.

I should've been focused on my own group.

Instead, I kept noticing things I probably shouldn't have.

The way Ava and Mia didn't avoid each other anymore, exactly.

The way they still paused before speaking, like there was an extra invisible question in every sentence.

The way Nolan had clearly realized he was stuck in the middle of something he didn't understand but had chosen to become professionally pleasant about it.

It was weirdly impressive.

When class ended, I stayed behind long enough to ask Ms. Howard a question about our assignment I absolutely could have figured out myself.

By the time I stepped into the hall, most people were gone.

Most.

Not all.

Connor was at the water fountain with two other boys from band, talking way too loudly.

"Seriously," he was saying, "if I liked somebody enough to send a public manifesto, I'd at least own it."

One of the other boys laughed.

The other one said, "That's because you need attention to live."

Connor grinned. "Exactly."

I stopped walking.

For one second, I just stood there.

And that was the moment I understood something annoying about myself.

I had spent the whole week thinking I was staying above it.

Not turning into Derek or Connor or whoever else had decided eighth grade was one long open-mic night for human nonsense.

But staying above it wasn't the same as doing anything useful.

Camila had said that already, in her deeply offensive wise older-sister way.

Still, hearing it at home and feeling it in a hallway were different things.

And right then, listening to Connor treat Mia like a punchline and this whole thing like his own private material, silence started feeling less neutral.

Lazier.

Connor saw me and lifted his chin. "Yo."

I met his eyes.

One of his friends immediately went quieter, which should have told him something.

It didn't.

"You good?" Connor asked, with a smirk that made the question rotten before it even landed.

There are people who know how to weaponize normal words.

Connor was one of them.

"No," I said.

That got rid of the smirk for about half a second.

He laughed. "Dang. Honest."

The other two boys didn't laugh.

I stepped closer.

Not in some movie-fight way.

Just enough that the whole thing stopped being casual.

"You need to stop," I said.

Connor blinked. "Stop what?"

"This."

I gestured between him, the hallway, the whole dumb atmosphere. "All of it."

He gave a short, fake-confused laugh. "Bro, I'm not even doing anything."

That was the exact sentence I was starting to hate most.

Not I'm just saying.

Not I'm not even doing anything.

I met his eyes for one second longer.

"You are, though," I said.

His friends looked at the floor.

Connor crossed his arms. "All right, so now you're what? Her bodyguard?"

I recognized it immediately.

The move.

Turn everything into a joke again.

Keep the ground loose so nobody had to stand still long enough to be real.

"No," I said. "I'm just tired of listening to you act like somebody else's worst week is your personality."

That one landed.

I could tell since Connor's face changed before he figured out how to recover it.

the other two boys looked embarrassed to be standing there with him, which honestly did more work than anything else.

One of them muttered, "We should go."

Connor didn't answer.

The second boy said, "Yeah," and the three of them moved off down the hall in this awkward little clump of unfinished swagger.

I stood there for another second after they left, heart beating harder than it should have for something that technically hadn't even been a fight.

I turned and almost ran into Ava.

She was standing six feet away with a folder tucked against her chest.

I had no idea how long she'd been there.

Long enough.

We looked at each other.

"That was weirdly intense," she said.

I exhaled. "Yeah."

Ava shifted the folder to her other arm. "Thanks."

That word again.

Everybody in this story suddenly saying thanks at the exact moments when it felt too small.

I rubbed the back of my neck. "He was being a jerk."

"He usually is."

"True."

She looked down the hallway where Connor had gone. "Still."

I gave one small nod.

Because I couldn't help myself, I said, "I should've said something sooner."

Ava looked back at me.

"You're not the reason any of this happened," she said.

"I know."

"You sound like you're arguing with yourself."

"That also sounds accurate."

The corner of her mouth moved, not quite into a smile.

She said, "It's just weird."

"Everything is weird."

"No, I mean…" She looked down. "I don't know how to explain it. I'm mad at Mia. I'm still mad. But people turning all of this into a joke somehow makes me want to defend her."

I met her eyes.

That was not what I expected her to say.

Ava gave a tiny shrug. "I know. Gross."

I laughed once.

She shook her head. "It's just—she was wrong. But this is still real. And they keep making it fake."

The best summary anybody had said yet.

Wrong.

But real.

I leaned against the wall beside the drinking fountain.

"That's what's annoying me too."

Ava looked down the emptying hallway. "It's like the second something becomes public; people act like it stops belonging to the actual people in it."

"That's probably the smartest thing anybody at this school has said in months."

"Don't sound so shocked."

"I'm not shocked. I'm impressed."

That actually got the smallest smile out of her.

The warning bell rang and the hallway refilled with movement.

We both straightened automatically.

Ava adjusted her backpack strap. "I should go."

"Yeah."

She took a step, then paused.

"You know she's having a really bad day, right?"

I met her eyes.

Ava's expression had closed up a little again, not cold exactly but protected.

"I'm not saying that means anything huge," she said. "I'm just saying. She looked awful in English."

I gave a slow nod.

Ava looked like she wanted to say one more thing.

Didn't.

She headed off toward the stairs.

I stood there until the late bell rang, then went to class.

The rest of the day felt off in that thin, tired way days do after you've already had the conversation you were supposed to avoid.

At lunch, Ryder asked me if I was coming to the park Saturday, and I said maybe.

Mateo asked if I wanted his extra granola bar, and I said no.

A teacher asked me to carry a stack of folders down to the office, and I did, mostly because walking through the building with a reason felt easier than walking through it as myself.

On the way back from the office, I passed the side bench by the gym and saw Mia sitting there alone.

No Becca.

No phone in her hand.

Just her backpack beside her and that specific look people get when they are trying very hard not to let their face show the full amount of what they're feeling.

She looked up when she heard my steps.

I slowed.

There are some moments where leaving would feel cowardly and staying would feel too pointed.

This was one of them.

So naturally I made the medium-bad choice and stopped.

"How's everything?" I asked.

The second it left my mouth; I almost took it back.

Mia looked at me for one second, and I could actually see her deciding whether to lie.

"Not great," she said.

That made me respect her a little more than I wanted to admit.

I glanced at the empty bench.

At her again.

"Can I sit?"

She gave a short, tired nod.

I sat down at the far end, same as before.

Neither of us said anything.

She held out a folded piece of paper.

I took it, opened it, and read:

ask jayden if he wants to help w ur project too lol

My whole face went flat.

"That's dumb," I said.

Mia laughed once under her breath. "You keep saying that like it's new information."

"It's still true."

She took the paper back and folded it smaller.

"I know people are going to talk," she said. "I know that. I'm not asking for some magical no-one-be-an-idiot force field."

"That would be useful, though."

"Extremely."

She looked down at the note in her hands. "I'm just tired of everything turning into one version."

Again.

Version.

Storyline.

Everybody in this school circling the same truth from different directions.

I leaned my elbows on my knees. "Then don't let the dumbest version win."

She looked at me.

I kept going before I could stop myself.

"You can't control whether people talk. But you don't have to start acting like their version explains you."

Mia was quiet.

Then: "You make that sound easy."

"It isn't."

"Good. Because I'm failing at it."

I gave one small nod. "Same."

That got her to glance over.

I shrugged. "People keep acting like I'm supposed to explain this whole thing with one sentence too."

She looked at me a little differently after that.

Not dramatically. Just less alone.

And for some reason, that made me realize how tired she actually looked.

Not just embarrassed.

Worn out.

Like she had spent a week trying to carry around too many interpretations of herself and had finally run out of room.

"I never thought your apology was fake," I said.

The words came out before I could reconsider them.

Mia blinked.

"What?"

"I said I never thought it was fake."

Her face changed slightly.

Like the sentence had landed in a place that was bruised.

"Thanks," she said quietly.

I shrugged. "Seemed worth saying."

The late-lunch bell rang inside.

I stood up first.

"I should go."

"Yeah."

I took a step, then looked back.

"For what it's worth," I said, "people being lazy about your motives doesn't mean they're right."

Mia looked up at me.

Nodded once.

I went back inside before I said anything else.

There was a line in this whole mess I was trying not to cross, and I still wasn't totally sure where it was.

After school, I ended up at the park anyway.

Ryder was there.

Mateo too.

A bunch of kids from different grades shooting baskets and pretending none of us lived inside the same school pressure cooker all week.

At one point Ryder bounced the ball to me and said, "You know what the weirdest part is?"

"That you ask questions like that with no warning?"

"No, about the Mia thing."

I groaned. "Of course."

He leaned on the fence. "No, listen. A week ago, everybody was talking about the text. Now everybody's talking about her apology, her crush, whether Ava's over it, whether you're over it, whether any of you are secretly whatever."

I caught the ball when Mateo threw it back and waited.

Ryder looked around the court. "It's not even one thing anymore."

Right there.

Finally.

The sentence I had been trying to build toward in my head for days.

"Exactly," I said.

Ryder blinked. "Wait. You agree with me?"

"Don't get all emotional."

Mateo laughed.

I bounced the ball once and looked toward the chain-link fence, past the park, toward the street where school lived in everybody's head even when we weren't there.

"It's not one rumor," I said. "It's like ten versions of the same thing, and people just keep passing around whichever one lets them feel involved."

Ryder frowned a little. "That was weirdly deep."

"Yeah, well. I'm having a weirdly deep week."

He nodded once. "Fair."

And that was it.

No big speech.

Just that small moment where even Ryder, king of saying the wrong thing at high speed, looked like he understood the shape of it for one second.

That night, I got home sore from the park and tired in a way that had nothing to do with basketball.

Camila was on the couch doing something on her laptop that looked serious enough to be fake homework and real enough to keep her from bothering me immediately.

I should've gone upstairs.

Instead, I stopped in the doorway and said, "You were right."

She looked up slowly.

"Oh wow," she said. "Should I write this down?"

"I hate you."

"No, you don't. Which part was I right about?"

I leaned against the doorframe. "The part where standing around being chill isn't neutral."

She stared at me.

Nodded once. "Yeah."

"That's all?"

She closed the laptop. "Jayden. When a room is full of people making something worse, the person who could help and doesn't is still shaping the room."

That sat with me.

The decision.

Not another apology.

Not another correction after the fact.

A decision, in the moment, not to let a bad version keep spreading just because the room made it easy.

I didn't say any of that out loud.

I just nodded once and headed upstairs.

On my bed later, phone in one hand, I hovered over the group chat without opening it.

At my messages.

At nothing.

The week had started with one bad message.

Now it felt like all of us were standing inside the echo of it, waiting to see who would finally be brave enough to stop the next one before it landed.

And finally, I had a feeling it might actually happen.

Enough Already

Mia:

By Monday, I was tired in a way sleep could not fix.

Not sleepy.

Just worn thin.

Like every conversation for the last week had taken a little strip off my nerves and by now there was nothing left between me and the world except hoodie fabric and bad posture.

The problem with surviving something embarrassing is that people start congratulating themselves for how normal they're acting while you're still trying to figure out how to exist in your own skin again.

By first period, two teachers had smiled at me in that careful way adults do when they think they're being reassuring and are actually just making you feel like a recovering zoo animal.

By second period, Connor had managed to say "project partner" in a tone that somehow sounded illegal.

By lunch, I had started seriously considering whether it was possible to transfer schools using only vibes and a fake permission slip.

"Mia."

I lifted my gaze.

Becca was standing over me with her tray and the expression of someone bracing for impact.

"What?"

"You've been glaring at your mashed potatoes for two minutes."

"That's because they know what they did."

She sat down across from me. "You seem extra weird today."

"Thank you."

"You're welcome."

That got the smallest possible eye roll out of me, which I think she counted as progress.

Around us, the cafeteria was loud in the usual way—plastic trays, shouted names, a dropped fork, somebody laughing too hard at something not funny enough to deserve it.

Ordinary lunch noise.

The kind that had started sounding fake lately.

Like school was trying to reassure me it was still school while secretly keeping a camera on my table at all times.

Becca opened her chocolate milk. "Are you still thinking about the note?"

"No."

That was a lie.

She gave me a look.

"Yes," I corrected.

"Thought so."

I stabbed a fry and then didn't eat it.

The note had been dumb.

That was true.

Jayden had said it.

Ava had said it differently.

Even Becca had said it in her own Becca way.

But the thing about dumb things is that they still get inside you if they hit the right bruise.

And that note had hit one perfectly.

It took everything messy and human and flattened it into one cheap explanation that made everybody else more comfortable.

"Mia."

I lifted my gaze again.

Becca had gone a little more serious.

"You know you don't have to act normal for me, right?"

I laughed once under my breath. "That is a dangerous offer."

"I'm brave."

"You're nosy."

"Yes, well that too."

For one second, I almost said something real.

Sophie slid into the seat at the end of the table without asking, and the moment died on impact.

"I have a question," she said.

Becca actually closed her eyes.

"No," she said.

Sophie frowned. "I didn't even ask it yet."

"That has literally never improved anything."

Sophie ignored her and looked at me. "Are you still doing the project with Ava?"

There was nothing technically wrong with the question.

That didn't help.

It was too normal.

"Yes," I said carefully.

"Oh."

That one syllable contained enough subtext to qualify as a hate crime.

I turned to her. "What does that mean?"

"Nothing."

School's national anthem.

Nothing.

Just saying.

No offense.

I set my fork down. "Then why say it like that?"

Sophie blinked. "I was just wondering if it was awkward."

Becca made a strangled noise. "Wow. Incredible recovery. Really smooth."

Sophie rolled her eyes. "I didn't mean anything bad."

I believed that, which made it more exhausting.

Half the problem at school wasn't maliciousness.

It was people treating other people's mess like open-source material.

Before I could answer, a voice from two tables over cut through the noise.

"Yo, Jayden!"

I turned.

Derek.

Naturally.

He was half-standing on the bench at his table since sitting like a person had never really appealed to him.

Jayden looked up from where he was sitting with Ryder and Mateo.

Derek grinned. "Need you to settle something."

Every muscle in my body tightened at once as if I knew what was coming next.

At Ava's table, Tessa had stopped talking.

Lila looked up.

Ava turned just slightly in her seat.

The whole room did not go quiet.

It did that thing again.

That thinning.

That subtle pulling-back of noise when a moment starts building its own gravity.

Jayden said, "No."

A smart answer.

A fast answer.

Should have been enough.

Derek laughed. "Come on, man. I'm just asking."

I hated that phrase so much by now it practically made my vision sharpen.

Ryder looked annoyed already.

Mateo looked tired.

Connor-from-band was turned halfway in his seat, openly listening.

Derek pointed vaguely between tables like human beings were geometry now. "If Mia hadn't said anything in the first place, would you and Ava have ever actually—"

He didn't get to finish as I stood up so fast my chair scraped hard across the floor.

And the sound of it cut through everything.

I did not think.

Or maybe I did, finally, just in a different order.

What hit me first wasn't panic.

It was recognition.

This was it.

The exact kind of moment I had kept arriving too late to.

The joke, half-made.

The rumor, halfway out of somebody's mouth.

The room, already bending toward the dumbest version.

And this time, I was there early enough to stop it before it landed.

"Don't," I said firmly.

I wasn't yelling.

I didn't need to be.

Derek looked at me, surprised.

A bunch of other people did too.

The whole cafeteria suddenly felt huge and close at the same time.

I could hear my own pulse in my ears.

Derek gave a short laugh, trying to put the moment back under his control. "What?"

"Don't do this again."

He blinked. "I was just asking—"

"No." My voice came out steadier this time. "You weren't. You were trying to turn it into a joke again."

Nobody moved.

Not Sophie.

Not Becca.

Not Connor.

Not even the lunch monitor by the vending machines, who was definitely aware something was happening and had decided to let the children self-destruct educationally.

Derek shrugged, still trying for casual. "It kind of is a joke at this point."

The line.

The exact line that split everything.

A week ago, I might have gone hot with embarrassment and let someone else say something.

Three days ago, I might have waited and corrected it afterward in some smaller, safer way.

Not now.

"No," I said. "It's not."

The words came out before I could soften them.

"You all keep acting like it's funny because then nobody has to think about what they're actually saying."

Derek's grin slipped.

Good.

I kept going.

Once the truth starts moving, it gets harder to stop than a lie.

"Ava didn't do anything," I said, louder now, not because I was giving a speech, but because if people were going to keep listening anyway, they might as well hear something useful. "Jayden didn't do anything. I heard something dumb, I repeated it, and I made it worse. That part was me."

I could feel the room on me.

Every face.

Every phone probably still sitting face-up on every table.

Every single awful possibility of this becoming yet another version by third period.

And still—

I didn't stop.

"So, if people are still talking about it now," I said, "then at this point you're choosing to be mean on purpose."

Nobody laughed.

Derek looked like he wanted to.

Or wanted to keep pretending this was light enough to survive his usual personality.

But he couldn't.

The room had changed.

He could feel it.

I could feel it.

Everybody could.

Ava was turned fully around in her seat now.

Jayden was standing.

I hadn't even seen him stand.

Ryder's expression had gone from interested to actually serious, which might have been the most shocking event of the entire month.

Derek's face went red under the fluorescent lights.

"Okay," he said finally, but it came out smaller than he probably wanted.

No joke after it.

No grin.

No bounce-back line.

Just okay.

And since the universe likes to make sure no one escapes these things looking graceful, the lunch monitor finally wandered over and said, "Is there a problem here?"

Nobody answered.

Derek sat down.

That was answer enough.

The lunch monitor looked around, sensed social radiation, and decided she did not get paid enough for detail.

"All right then," she said. "Keep it respectful."

Becca made a tiny choking sound beside me that I'm pretty sure was a laugh trying not to exist.

The room started moving again after that.

Somebody picked up a tray.

A chair scraped.

The noise level rose back to normal.

Connor looked away first, which felt important for reasons I couldn't fully explain.

And then I made the mistake of realizing I was still standing in the middle of all of it.

Every part of me went hot all at once.

I sat down too fast.

My hands were shaking.

Not visibly, I hoped.

But enough that I shoved them under the table immediately.

Becca stared at me.

"What?" I whispered.

She blinked. "I think you just had a moment."

"That sounds terrible."

"It was kind of incredible."

"Do not say incredible right now."

"I'm serious."

Across the room, I could feel Ava still looking at me.

I did not look back.

Not yet.

I knew if I did, my face would do something human and unhelpful.

Sophie was staring too, but in a much less important way.

She leaned toward me and said quietly, "I wasn't trying to make it worse earlier."

I met her eyes.

That was new.

"I know," I said.

And I did.

That was part of why all of this had gotten so exhausting.

A lot of people weren't trying to be cruel.

They were just willing to be careless.

Again, and again and again.

And eventually the effect was the same.

Lunch ended in a blur after that.

I barely tasted anything.

Couldn't have told you what was on my tray if someone offered me money.

As people started standing up, Becca leaned toward me.

"For the record," she said, "if anyone ever writes the official history of eighth grade, I need it noted that I was there for that."

I gave her a look.

She put a hand over her heart. "Witnessed it live. Very moving."

That got the faintest involuntary breath-laugh out of me.

Which I resented.

But only slightly.

In the hallway after lunch, I was halfway to math when somebody said my name behind me.

Not loudly.

Just: "Mia."

Ava.

I turned.

Tessa and Lila were with her, but both had slowed back a little in that obvious friend way that says we are technically here, but emotionally this is above our pay grade.

Ava stopped in front of me.

For one second neither of us said anything.

She said, "You didn't have to do that."

That was such an Ava sentence.

Not thank you.

Just something hovering sideways between all of them.

"Yes, I did," I said.

She looked at me.

Nodded once.

That tiny nod landed harder than the entire cafeteria had.

Lila was pretending very hard not to watch from three feet away.

Tessa was pretending less hard, but with more dignity.

Ava shifted her backpack strap higher. "Still."

That landed.

Her version of thank you.

I nodded back.

There should have been more.

A bigger scene.

A cleaner exchange.

Something that would feel satisfying and chapter-ending and emotionally legible.

Instead, the bell rang.

Ava stepped back.

"I'll see you in English," she said.

And then she was gone with Tessa and Lila, and I was left standing in the hallway with my heart doing something medically unnecessary and a bunch of seventh graders pushing around me like none of that had just happened.

Math was useless.

I got one equation wrong three different ways, which honestly felt creative.

Connor-from-band didn't look at me once in fourth period, which I counted as both a miracle and a personal achievement.

By the end of the day, the whole school seemed quieter around me.

Not in a dramatic respect way.

More like people had realized the topic had grown sharp edges and were less interested in handling it barehanded.

That alone felt like progress.

Outside by the buses, I saw Jayden before he saw me.

He was with Ryder, but not really listening to him.

When he looked up and caught my eye, he didn't smile.

He just gave the smallest nod.

Like: *yes.*

You did that.

I saw it.

I nodded back before I could overthink it.

Immediately wished human communication had less forehead involvement.

On the bus ride home, I sat by the window and let the motion of the road shake some of the leftover adrenaline loose.

Finally in days, I didn't feel like I had corrected something after it was already on fire.

This time, I'd stepped in before the version got bigger.

It hadn't been perfect.

And I certainly hadn't done it gracefully.

My chair had practically announced itself to the room like a legal warning.

But still.

I had done it.

And the weirdest part was, I didn't even feel better in the clean, relieved way I thought I might.

I felt wrung out.

Embarrassed.

Still shaky.

But underneath that—

Less trapped.

Like I had finally acted from the version of myself I'd been trying to get back to all week, instead of just chasing her after the fact.

When I got home, my mom was in the kitchen slicing cucumbers with the calm energy of someone who did not yet know her daughter had nearly started a cafeteria revolution before algebra.

"How was school?" she asked.

I dropped my backpack by the wall.

"Complicated."

She looked over her shoulder. "That usually means interesting."

I thought about the cafeteria.

Derek's face.

Ava's nod.

The way the room had changed when I stopped waiting for somebody else to be decent first.

I said, "I think I did the right thing."

My mom set the knife down and turned.

There was a pause.

She smiled a little.

"That feels important," she said.

"Yeah."

I leaned against the counter and looked down at my hands.

They were steady now.

Finally all day.

And that, more than anything, made me realize something had shifted.

Not the whole story.

Not all at once.

But the direction of it.

At the beginning of the week, I had used words like a weapon because I was angry and scared and wanted somebody to agree with me.

Today I used them because nobody else was stopping the same old garbage from growing another head.

That didn't erase anything.

But maybe nothing was going to erase it.

Maybe the best I could do was stop making myself smaller than the truth when the moment actually mattered.

That night, just before bed, my phone buzzed once.

A text from Ava.

Only three words.

that meant something

The screen held me there for a long time.

Typed back:

good

I almost added more.

Deleted it.

This time, more didn't feel necessary.

Maybe three honest words were enough to carry a whole day.

The New Norm

Ava:

People kept looking at me like I held the final answer.

Not just Tessa and Lila, though definitely them.

Not just random people in the hallway either, with their weird little sideways glances like they were checking whether my face had turned into a public statement.

Everybody.

Mia had stood up in the cafeteria and said what she said, and now everyone seemed to think I was supposed to know what it meant.

I didn't.

That was the issue.

But it also wasn't one of those magical movie moments where the right speech fixes all the emotional plumbing and then everybody's friendship comes back shinier than before.

Life was rude enough not to work like that.

At my locker after last period, Tessa leaned against the one next to mine and said, "Okay."

I kept stuffing books into my backpack. "No."

"I didn't even say anything yet."

"Yes, you did. You said okay in that voice."

Tessa pressed her lips together, which was always a bad sign.

Lila came up on my other side like they were trying to corner a squirrel that also happened to be their best friend.

"Come on," Lila said. "Just tell us what you're thinking."

I shut my locker.

Too hard, probably.

"Why?" I asked. "So, you can hold a post-game analysis?"

Tessa winced. "Ouch."

"Sorry," I said automatically.

Since honesty was ruining all of our lives lately, I added, "No, actually. Not sorry."

That got a brief laugh out of Lila.

"Fair," she said.

We started walking toward the buses, and for half a block nobody said anything. Which, with Tessa and Lila, counted as either deep respect or temporary system failure.

Lila said, carefully, "It mattered."

I met her eyes.

She shrugged one shoulder. "What Mia did."

Tessa nodded. "Yeah."

I looked ahead at the buses lined up at the curb.

"I know."

They both glanced at me.

"What?" I asked.

Tessa tilted her head. "You sound mad at that."

I exhaled. "I'm not mad at that."

"What are you mad at, then?" Lila asked.

Everything, I almost said.

Instead, I said, "I'm mad that now I have to have feelings about it."

Tessa laughed once under her breath. "That is probably the most honest answer you've given all week."

Unfortunately, yes.

That was exactly it.

If Mia had stayed defensive, or dramatic, or self-pitying, or just generally committed to making everything worse, then my life would actually be simpler.

I could stay on the side of the story where I knew who had done what and why it mattered.

But standing up in the cafeteria and shutting Derek down before he got to make me into the joke again?

That complicated things.

It was the kind of thing you do when you mean it.

When you are willing to take the hit instead of waiting for the room to decide whether cruelty counts as fun.

At the bus line, Tessa bumped my shoulder lightly.

"You don't owe anybody instant forgiveness," she said.

I met her eyes.

She shrugged. "What? I can be emotionally competent sometimes."

"Rarely," Lila said.

"Wow," Tessa said. "Attacked in public."

I smiled a little despite myself.

I glanced toward the far side of the bus lane and saw Mia.

She was standing with Becca, phone in one hand, backpack on one shoulder, looking less panicked than she had been earlier and more… drained.

Like all the adrenaline had burned out and left her with nothing but gravity.

She looked up.

Saw me.

Stopped.

I stopped too.

Not physically.

Just internally.

That was the thing now.

Every time we looked at each other, it felt like some invisible door had to decide whether it was opening or closing.

Mia didn't wave.

She didn't smile.

She just held my gaze for one second longer than strangers would.

Looked away.

And I got on the bus.

At home, my mom was in the kitchen stirring something in a pot that smelled like tomatoes and garlic and the kind of dinner that would have been comforting if my life had not recently become one long social autopsy.

"How was school?" she asked.

I dropped my backpack by the door. "Okay."

She looked over. "That sounds familiar."

I sat at the counter and pulled a stray thread from my hoodie sleeve. "Mia said something in the cafeteria."

My mom turned the stove down a little. "Good something or bad something?"

I thought about it.

That should have been an easy question to answer.

It wasn't.

"Good," I said finally. "I think."

She waited.

Parents are so good at waiting. It's one of their worst qualities.

"She stopped Derek when he started making it into a joke again," I said. "Like… right away."

My mom nodded slowly.

Not even a question.

I made a face. "I literally just said that."

"No," she said. "You literally said good, I think. Which is not the same thing."

I rested my chin in my hand. "I hate when everybody is reasonable."

My mom smiled a little. "No, you don't."

"No," I admitted. "I really don't."

She came around the counter and sat across from me.

"Do you want my opinion?" she asked.

Not really.

"Yes," I said.

She folded her hands loosely. "It sounds like Mia did something right. Like she's trying to make up for her mistakes."

My gaze dropped to the counter.

"That doesn't erase what she did wrong before," my mom added. "Those can both be true."

I gave one small nod.

Yes.

That was the exact problem.

It would be easier if growth erased damage.

If apologies replaced hurt.

If one good moment canceled one bad one like points in a game.

But this wasn't a game.

It was just people.

And people were rude enough to stay complicated.

"I don't know what I'm supposed to do with that," I said.

My mom tilted her head. "Why do you need to do anything with it right now?"

I lifted my gaze.

She smiled a little, not unkindly. "Ava, understanding something is not the same as being required to wrap it up neatly like a gift wrapped package."

That made me want to throw a spoon in a respectful way.

It was exactly what I needed to hear and therefore deeply irritating.

After dinner, I went upstairs with my phone and my homework and completed exactly fourteen percent of the homework before opening my messages instead.

Tessa had sent: ***u alive***

Lila had sent: ***if u dont answer im assuming u ran away to canada***

I typed back: ***cant im too close to the border of idaho and thats not aspirational enough***

Tessa immediately replied: ***fair***

Then: ***serious question tho***

do u think u and mia are ever gonna be normal again

The screen glowed back at me.

Locked my phone.

I genuinely did not know.

The weird thing was, a week ago I would have said we already were normal.

Not best friends.

Not enemies.

Just… Neighbors.

History.

A shared orbit.

Enough familiarity to glide over the awkward parts and call it fine.

Now I could see that normal had mostly been us avoiding the truth in a socially acceptable way.

And once you saw that, it was hard to unsee.

A message came in from Mia before I could decide whether to answer Tessa.

Her name sat there on the screen.

Opened it.

sorry if that was too much today

I read it twice.

That was very Mia.

Not I'm glad I said it.

Not Did you hear me?

Not Please say I did the right thing.

Just: sorry if that was too much.

Always somehow apologizing for the shape of herself after the fact.

I typed: ***it wasnt***

That took a second to land.

Added: ***it was the first time u didnt wait until after***

That felt like the truest thing I could say.

The typing bubbles appeared almost immediately.

Disappeared.

Came back.

Then: ***yeah***

i know

The screen glowed back at me.

There was something about that answer that got to me.

It sounded like she understood what I meant without trying to make herself sound wiser than she was.

I typed: ***that was important***

I sent it before I could overthink it into something safer and less useful.

This time the pause on her side was longer.

Then: ***okay***

That made me smile a little.

I set my phone down and looked across my room.

At the lamp.

The chair with clothes thrown over it.

The stack of books by the wall.

Normal life things.

The same normal life I'd been trying to get back to all week.

I wasn't sure normal was what I wanted anymore.

Not the old version.

Not the one where Mia and I drifted around each other pretending that old history was enough to cover all the new tension.

Not the one where one of us could quietly resent the other and the other one could quietly feel it and both of us kept showing up to each other's lives like nothing had changed.

Maybe normal wasn't the goal.

Maybe honest was.

That thought sat with me while I brushed my teeth and while I climbed into bed and while the lights from cars moved in slow strips across the ceiling.

Three houses away, Mia's room light clicked off around the same time mine did.

I noticed. Obviously, I did.

The neighborhood was too small not to notice things like that.

And that was another part of the problem, maybe.

Not just that Mia and I had history.

That our lives were still physically arranged to keep brushing against each other whether we were ready or not.

School.

Sidewalk.

Driveways.

Moms.

Project groups chosen by people with no apparent respect for emotional boundaries.

It meant there was no dramatic ending available to us.

No clean split.

No movie version where one person walks away into a different life.

There was only this:

the next conversation.

The next choice.

The next time one of us could either tell the truth or hide behind something easier.

And maybe that was why the cafeteria thing mattered more than I wanted it to.

It wasn't just Mia defending me.

It was Mia not hiding.

Not waiting.

Not making herself smaller than the truth to protect her own comfort.

That was new.

Or maybe it had always been in her somewhere and I just hadn't seen it clearly in a while.

Either way, it changed the shape of what came next.

I still wasn't over it.

I was still hurt.

Still angry in certain corners of myself.

Still not interested in pretending this had all become some inspiring friendship lesson sponsored by the English department.

But finally, I could actually imagine a version of the future that wasn't built entirely out of stiffness.

Not old normal.

Not instant repair.

Just something more honest than what we had before.

And weirdly enough, that felt harder.

But also, better.

Different But Good

Mia:

By Friday, nothing was fixed.

That was the first true thing.

The second true thing was that everything was different anyway.

School still looked the same. Same lockers. Same flicky light by the science wing that nobody ever repaired. Same cafeteria pizza with the structural integrity of wet cardboard. Same buses lined up outside like giant yellow reminders that eighth grade was not, in fact, optional.

But the week didn't sit on me the same way anymore.

At the beginning of all this, every hallway had felt like a trap.

Now they mostly just felt like hallways again.

Just ordinary enough that I could walk through them without bracing for impact every three steps.

That was progress, I guessed.

Or maybe just exhaustion wearing better shoes.

I was at my locker before first period, switching out books I wouldn't read for books I'd also probably pretend to read, when Ava stopped beside me.

I lifted my gaze.

She had one strap of her backpack over her shoulder and that calm expression she used when she was trying not to let the whole room into her actual thoughts.

"Hey," she said.

Just that.

The word that had done more emotional labor than any other in the English language.

"Hey," I said back.

For one second, I thought maybe that was it.

Maybe we were both just trying out what normal politeness sounded like after social catastrophe.

She held out a folded paper.

I went still.

"What's that?"

"Our final English outline," she said. "Nolan wanted me to make sure you got the updated version before class."

I took it.

Our fingers brushed.

Which should not have meant anything, except lately every tiny human interaction felt like it arrived with subtitles.

"Oh," I said. "Thanks."

Ava nodded.

Before I could get stuck in my own head about whether now was the time to say something significant, she said, "Also, for the record, your conclusion slide was better than Nolan's."

I blinked once.

"That feels illegal to tell me."

"It's just true."

"That's honestly huge."

One corner of her mouth moved.

Not quite a smile.

Possibly a smirk.

Still.

She said, "Don't make it weird."

I met her eyes.

"You literally walked up to my locker and complimented my slide."

"Exactly," she said. "And now you're in danger of making it weird."

That got me.

A real laugh, quick and surprised.

Ava looked at me, and finally in what felt like forever, the space between us didn't tighten immediately.

It didn't loosen all the way either.

But it didn't tighten.

Becca came around the corner, saw both of us standing there, and made a visible effort not to react with her whole face.

Which was truly one of the nicest things she'd ever done for me.

"Morning," she said, in the exaggerated tone of someone trying very hard to sound like nothing in the world was remotely notable.

"Morning," Ava said.

I said it too.

For one weird second the three of us just stood there in a triangle made entirely of social history and bad technology.

The warning bell rang and saved us all from becoming too self-aware before 8:00 a.m.

Ava headed toward class.

Becca watched her go, then looked at me.

"That seemed… promising?"

I slid the folded outline into my binder. "Do not narrate my life to me."

"I'm not narrating. I'm observing."

"You are absolutely narrating."

She considered. "You got me."

We started walking.

She bumped my shoulder lightly and said, "For what it's worth, you seem less haunted."

I met her eyes.

She lifted one shoulder. "Still haunted. Just… not in a Victorian-child-by-the-window way."

"That is unbelievably specific."

"It's a gift."

English went fine.

Actually fine.

Nolan talked too much, our slides worked, Ava gave her points cleanly, and when it was my turn to do the close, my voice only shook in one place, which I decided was practically professional.

After class, Ms. Howard told us our group worked well together, which felt like hearing a wedding officiant compliment the seating chart at a disaster reception.

Still, I took the win.

By lunch, the whole week had started to feel less like an active fire and more like the smell after one.

Still there.

Just not taking up all the oxygen anymore.

I sat down with Becca and actually ate my food, which she noticed immediately because my appetite had become a tracked event.

"Wow," she said. "Chewing. We love to see it."

"Please never say that again."

"No promises."

Across the cafeteria, Jayden was standing by the trash cans talking to Ryder and Mateo.

At some point a week ago, looking in his direction would have felt like triggering a silent alarm in my own body.

Now it mostly felt like noticing a person I knew.

But less catastrophic.

Like my feelings had finally been demoted from national emergency to private inconvenience.

He looked over.

Caught me looking.

And instead of everything inside me trying to leave my body through my pores, I just held the look for one second and lifted my hand in the smallest possible wave.

Not weird.

Just human.

Jayden nodded back once.

That was all.

Becca saw the whole thing, obviously, because Becca would notice a leaf changing emotional direction from fifty yards away.

She slowly turned back to me. "Interesting."

"Quiet."

"I said one word."

"It was a loud word."

She grinned and opened her chips.

At the end of the day, I walked home instead of taking the bus.

Why not? After the week I'd had, movement felt easier than sitting in rows while everyone pretended not to have opinions.

The neighborhood looked painfully normal.

A bike lying in someone's yard.

A dog barking behind a fence.

A little kid drawing with chalk on the sidewalk like public humiliation wasn't even on the list of things the world had invented yet.

I passed Ava's house first.

Her mom's car was in the driveway.

A package sat by the front step.

The porch light wasn't on yet.

The usual things.

I got to mine.

My mom was kneeling by the flower bed out front, digging around in the dirt like she had a personal issue with weeds.

She looked up when she saw me. "You walked."

"Yeah."

"How was school?"

I thought about that.

Really thought about it.

About the cafeteria.

About the apology.

About the note.

About Ava at my locker this morning.

About Becca trying very hard not to make every serious moment into a podcast.

About Jayden being normal enough to make that feel strange.

About how none of it was erased.

How all of it still mattered.

And still—

"Better," I said.

My mom sat back on her heels and looked at me.

She smiled a little. "That sounds positive."

"It is."

I dropped my backpack by the porch and sat on the front step.

My mom brushed dirt off her hands and came over, sitting one step above me.

Neither of us said anything for a minute.

The street hummed quietly around us. Somewhere farther down, a garage door opened. A breeze pushed through the trees hard enough to make the branches rattle a little.

Finally, my mom asked, "What did you learn?"

I exhaled.

That was such a parent question.

Also, such an impossible one to answer.

But I knew the one anyway.

"That being embarrassed isn't the same thing as being sorry," I said.

She nodded once.

"And that saying something in private doesn't make it harmless."

Another nod.

"And that if I'm already mad at someone, I can make myself believe a worse version of them way too fast."

That one came out quieter.

My mom didn't rush to fill the silence after it.

Good.

I wasn't done.

"And…" I picked at a loose thread on my sleeve. "I think I learned that normal isn't always good."

She tilted her head. "What do you mean?"

I looked across the street.

At nothing, really.

At everything.

"Before all this, me and Ava were normal," I said. "At least I thought we were. But really, we were just... used to each other. Used to not saying stuff."

My mom was quiet.

"I don't think I want that version back," I said.

Saying it out loud felt strange.

My mom rested her forearms on her knees. "What do you want instead?"

I thought about Ava's text.

that meant something

I thought about the library.

The hallway.

The locker this morning.

The way honest now felt harder than easy used to.

"Something real," I said.

My mom smiled a little. "That seems like a good place to start."

We sat there a while longer until the light started to change and the street went from afternoon to evening without asking anyone's permission.

Later, upstairs, I opened my phone and stared at Ava's name for a long time before typing.

It wasn't this huge paragraph.

I wasn't preparing a speech.

There was no apology spiral.

Just:

thx for today

and for not making the slide thing weird

I looked at it for one second.

Sent it.

She answered a minute later.

u did enough weird for both of us this week

That took a second to process.

Laughed out loud in my room by myself like a person who maybe had not fully lost everything after all.

I typed back:

fair

Then:

still

A longer pause.

Then:

Yeah

still

I set the phone down beside me and lay back on my bed.

Three houses away.

That was all.

Not a dramatic ending.

Not a giant reunion.

Just three houses.

One long week.

One terrible message.

A bunch of smaller true things said afterward.

The text I sent out, was a huge mistake on my part.

A bunch of smaller trues were then revealed afterward.

Now, instead of wanting to erase the entire thing, I weirdly wanted to remember it.

Not the humiliating parts.

Not Connor's face or Derek's jokes or the note folded in my binder like evidence from a crime scene.

I wanted to remember what it showed me. What I had learned from the experience.

That words count before they're public.

That gossip grows even when nobody thinks they're the one feeding it.

That sometimes the worst thing you do drags something honest into the light with it.

And that if you wait too long to tell the truth, eventually the room fills up with easier versions.

I had done that once.

I didn't think I'd do it the same way again.

Outside my window, the neighborhood had gone mostly dark.

Ava's porch light clicked on.

Ours.

Two small pools of yellow light on the same street.

Separate.

Visible.

Still there.

And that, I thought, was probably the closest thing to an ending, life ever actually gave you.

It wasn't perfect.

Just lit enough to keep going.

Thank You for Reading!

I sincerely hope you enjoyed this story.

I started writing books to create fast-paced, engaging stories that would encourage kids—including my own—to spend a little more time reading and a little less time staring at screens. Knowing that readers are enjoying these adventures means the world to me.

If you have a moment, I'd truly appreciate it if you left a quick review on Amazon. Even a short review helps other readers discover the book and encourages me to keep writing more stories.

Thank you for your support, and I hope you'll join me for another adventure soon.

– Adam Hunter

www.ingramcontent.com/pod-product-compliance
Lightning Source LLC
LaVergne TN
LVHW030921080826
845145LV00013B/2991

9781971734088